Home Guard

by

S. R. Port

Homecoming

As the plane door opens before me and the whine and whir of the airport greets me, hand-in-hand with the long absent bite of British air, I know that it is going to be strange to live without a face.

I lift my bag to my shoulder and slowly make my way up the tunnel to the terminal. Other passengers swarm past me with blank faces, but I have to carefully place each and every step to make sure I do not fall down. That would be embarrassing. Why don't they install handrails in these tunnels? It would make life so much easier for so many. I wouldn't have to move like a snail, leaning my hand against the wall like a drunkard. I've already been given some glances by other passengers, most of them in a strange new expression falling somewhere between nervous concern and sneering derision.

The usual scrum for immigration greets me, no

different here than any number of places in which I've arrived over the past ten years.

Ten years.

Jesus, has it really been ten years since I set foot in this airport, since I last set foot on this island? It suddenly seems far longer than it has before and the queue for the immigration desks stretches out even further, telescoping away in dizzying fashion. I am grasped by an acute feeling of anxiety. Is this going to work? Was Dram right to even suggest this?

I stagger for a moment. A man nearby sees me and reaches out to help. I manage to catch myself and reach out to indicate that I do not need his assistance.

"I'm sorry, th-thank you, I'm okay," I stammer.

The man smiles a little and turns away. I catch the woman he is with saying something that sounds like "sloshed", but I don't mind. Incorrect assumptions cannot hurt unless we let them, and it is ultimately by our actions that we are defined. Telling myself this, I try to draw up to my full height and hold on to whatever dignity I can.

Up ahead the officials are opening more desks and the

queue is separating into new rows of weary people. I edge to the left, eager to be away from the couple who have noticed me.

That familiar biting wind hits me again as the doors to the bus depot slide open. It is early – barely 6am – and even now in early summer the air is frigid. I welcome it, even grinning as it rushes across my non-face.

Hello, old friend. I've missed you.

The bus depot is bathed in the gloom of early morning. A grey pall of clouds covers everything, as it always seems to at Heathrow. Grey sky and grey concrete; Grey faces and grey spirits. No sort of welcome for a homecoming but I won't let it threaten my hopes, no matter how bad I may feel. Edging forwards I make my way along the railings by the side of the road to the bay indicated on the ticket I have purchased in haste after coming through the arrivals area. The sooner I can leave this place behind the better.

The bus pulls in twenty minutes later and I climb aboard, slowly moving along the aisle to the back seats. Few of my fellow passengers pay attention to this hunched, snail-slow invalid making his way to the isolation at the rear of the bus – after all, he has no face. Without a point of reference, something to hold on to and recognise, a man becomes less than a man. I am a shifting in the air, a ripple in the light and nothing more. For now, I suppose, there is some comfort in that.

Curled up in the seat, I watch the countryside fly past as we tear away from the capital. The distinctive southern landscape – all rolling hills and fields of crops for miles – whips by, frequently disappearing behind the raised verges that flank the motorway. Through the clouds in the distance, the sun forces rays of light which linger a while and then surrender to the overcast that surrounds them. There seems to be no real threat of rain, nor of sunshine. I am home.

My companions – I should say fellow travellers – are as faceless as I am, though neither in a literal sense, nor to the depths I find myself submerged in my own private world. They doze or stare out of the window, smartphones in hand and earphones in ear canals, giving me the space and time I need to feel completely apart.

It is a peculiar situation, I realise, to both lament and desire solitude and isolation in equal measure simultaneously. Or perhaps it is not. Perhaps you too have felt this sensation. I have read that prolonged isolation can intensify this feeling and I must say I can see the truth in that. What began for me as a painful and stressful experience has mutated over time; Sorrow at being alone became accepted, even embraced. One cannot simply give in and refuse to function. Greater introversion followed and has now even created fear of association – a kind of fear, at least. I would not avoid people, indeed I find conversation most agreeable and a worthy way of spending my time. No, I would not say I am afraid of my fellow man, but – given my history – I do feel a surprising fragility in my dealings with the rest of the world.

So, yes, peculiar, I suppose. I realise that I will have to tell you all eventually. It would be completely pointless for me to talk forever in this obtuse manner, without filling in the gaps in your knowledge of my situation. But that can wait. Indeed, it must wait and I beg you not to press me on the matter. I will explain all in my own time, I assure you.

For now, let us focus on the immediate facts of my situation. I am on a bus, bound for Oxford. Why Oxford, I cannot tell you, because I do not know myself. It just seemed like a nice idea as I looked through the bus timetable. I've not been there since my childhood and I would love to take it all in through the mature eyes of adulthood. A child can never grasp the gravity of a place, the weight of history and significance in the flagstones and towers, in the arches and spires. A child exists only in its own moment, only in and for itself. The greater purpose is only grasped through the gift of time and intelligence.

In contrast to my expectations, the cloud begins to disperse as we roll into the wooded undulations of the Oxfordshire countryside. Hints of blue become wide openings of clear sky and thin beams of sunlight broaden, bathing the verdant green of the land in a golden glow and reflecting off the surface of the Thames as we wind our way into the city. By the time we pull into Gloucester Green bus station in the heart of Oxford, summer feels and looks the part.

I wait until all the other passengers have alighted and then slowly feel my way down the central aisle to the pavement. I squint a little in the light. The windows in the bus must have been tinted and my eyes are unprepared for the intensity of the sunlight on the street.

People hurry to and fro around me, boarding other buses or making their way to one of the two exits nearby. I shuffle after a few of them, out onto George Street and into the middle of a huge throng of tourists. I have not seen such numbers of people in one place together since Jakarta and I find the experience quite dizzying. Every nationality under the sun must be represented on the streets of Oxford today and I catch snatches of countless different languages, only about half of which I recognise. What it is to be back in a cosmopolitan city in a cosmopolitan land; Simultaneously unsettling and invigorating, strange and familiar.

Leaving the horde to its thronging, I cross the road and catch the first bus out of the city, in the direction of the town of Carterton. There is no real system to my choice of bus or route, I just know that I would like to get some time alone in the country. I decide to ride the bus until a boarding house, hotel or inn takes my fancy and I can plan my next move from there.

My new bus slowly crawls out of Oxford, squashed in with hundreds of other vehicles on the city's woefully overburdened roads until we turn off into the countryside and race away, free. It is late morning by this time and the sun is rising towards its zenith. The earlier clouds have passed, leaving the land awash with beautiful light. On either side of us there are the gentle inclines of a river valley, broad fields of ripening wheat rippling like a sea in the breeze, rising to dense woodland atop the hills. Turning further west, through the centre of the valley, we pass between meadows of tall grasses, green, golden and brown, thistles and brambles, where cows slowly graze in the warm sun; Here and there I can see rabbits scurrying to burrows beneath the knotted protection of the blackberry bushes.

Very slowly, a smile broadens across my face and the weight in my forehead and chest lightens for a while. I lift my head a little to breathe in the air rushing through the windows at the top of the bus. In those few gulps I catch forgotten moments; The green aroma of the tree tops, the scent of flowers and grasses, the faint and not unwelcome whiff of manure and cow dung – does sunlight itself have a smell? It may sound absurd but I fancy I can even smell those rays, bouncing back from and passing through the foliage that surrounds me.

Out of the fields we roll, crossing a small toll bridge over the Thames and arriving in a small village centre, the very picture of rural life with its thatched cottages and market square, its stone-built homes and its thick-beamed public houses. Just beyond a beautiful Anglican church near the market square, I notice a sign for rooms and ring the bell to stop the bus. The next stop is only slightly further up the road and I step down from the bus at a pace that surprises me when I think back on it. The bus pulls away and I am left alone in the quiet street.

"G'afternoon," the man behind the bar of the Eagle Inn says warmly as I enter its dim interior. He is a stocky man of, I'd guess, about thirty-eight or nine, with slightly curled brown hair cut close to his head and a relaxed expression. I smile back at him and glance around at the room.

"Afternoon," I reply. "Business good?"

He laughs and gestures around the empty bar area.

"I'm rushed off me feet!" he chuckles in a voice that sounds like he may come from Cork or somewhere nearby. "Nah," he laughs again, "it'll pick up later, you can be sure of that. It's a Thursday, after all."

"The sign outside says you have vacant rooms," I say fumbling a little – I suddenly feel uneasy again. "Um...do you?"

"We sure do," he replies, pulling an old ledger up from behind the counter and laying it on the top of the bar. "Fifty pound a night for a single," he leans forwards and peers as if to look behind me. "If that's what you need."

"No," I say quickly, at which he frowns. "I mean 'yes'....I mean I'm alone."

"Right you are," he says, smiling again. "And how long do you think you'll be staying?"

"I don't really know," I say quietly.

"Right you are," he says again, "I'll put you down for a week then, if that's all right with you."

"Fine," I say and put my bag down on a chair near the

bar. He scribbles some details down in the book. As he does, I peer around the pub. It's a fairly ordinary interior to an attractive building and I cannot help but feel a little disappointed. A plaque above the bar proudly claims that the Eagle has been in operation since 1582, and there are certainly some old-looking beams above me, but otherwise there is little to indicate the age of the place. It appears to be yet another victim of a well-meaning but poorly-considered refit and lacks much in the way of charm.

Still the landlord – assuming this man is he – is friendly and welcoming and at least the place *smells* right. That incomparable mixture of beer and hops and nuts and wood; I can almost feel the tackiness of the tabletops. That, at least, is enough to bring a smile back to my face.

The man concludes his scribblings and looks up at me. "Okay, you'll be in number five and I'll give you thirty percent off, as you'll be here for a while."

"Thanks very much," I say, reaching for my bag. "Which way are the rooms?"

He throws his arms wide and gives me a mock incredulous look.

"Plenty time for that, y'bollocks! Sit down and have a pint on the house. Lager or ale for you?"

I am taken aback for a moment before I realise that he is being a good chap and smile at him.

"Ale for me, please," I say.

"Good man," he grins. "Take a seat."

The sun sets far later than I remember. Through the open window of my small room a cool breeze comes creeping, carrying with it the lingering scent of the fields and trees. Through the wide gap I have left between the curtains I watch swifts arcing and pirouetting in the air, backed by the deep oranges, pinks and blues of the painting that is the sky. Vast streaks of colour burn and merge above the silent land; Strokes of sky brushes in gifted hands. I lay in the dying light and listen for sounds outside. A dog barking occasionally, a village bus winding its way down empty streets now and again, the muttered chatter of the last of the Eagle's clientele making its way home – and behind all of it the distant, gentle whisper of the breeze in the treetops, rocking us all to sleep.

Dawn

I awake to the same sound as lulled me to sleep, yet for a moment, I do not know where I am. I stare upwards at the ceiling, its white paint job haphazardly splodged in places, as though holes have been hurriedly putty-filled beneath. Somewhere in the distance a dog barks and from above my head – my room is in a converted attic – I can hear a pigeon softly warbling.

Who-who...who...

Who-who....(?)

The room is bare and well-worn, to be sure, but there is charm in it as well. The floral patterns on the curtains and bedspread are different and match rather poorly – one being something like scarlet in hue, while the other is a faded orange – but they were clearly combined intentionally and some thoughtful soul has added some lavender in a pot to the bedside table in an attempt to restore some kind of balance. A picture hangs above the bed, rather incongruously portraying a coastal scene; Fishermen haul their boats onto a shingle beach, white surf breaking below a forbidding, stormy sky. Darren, the landlord, told me that he previously owned an inn on the East Anglia coast and I would not be surprised if this picture moved with him. It's an odd choice of image, cold and desolate, and yet through that it probably helps people appreciate the cosiness of the Eagle's rooms. Again, it has its charm.

I dress slowly, still unable to move that quickly and finding my trousers in particular to be a pain. My right small toe catches a little in the hem at the bottom of the trouser leg and the effort required to extract it still exhausts me. I have to sit for a while to rest again before I can brave the small en-suite bathroom to brush my teeth. It frustrates me immensely that I feel like this when I was once so active and strong. The wound in my shoulder is no longer causing any of my fatigue; This is completely psychological – or is it neurological? It's never been properly explained, or rather, it is something I have never bothered to ask. Still, the effect is clear and for all the improvement I have made, the deleterious pressure from my mind remains.

I promised before to explain something of my situation – well, I promised everything, but let's sleep on that. For now, let me describe myself. You might be wondering how old I am, given my physical difficulties and the like. I assure you that I am in my late thirties, no older than that. My present physical misfortunes will hopefully not be permanent and are, as mentioned, more the product of mental stress than any serious deterioration of my body. Although my stooping, stumbling and slow movement may divert attention from the fact, I am a handsome sort, in my own way. My dark brown hair and beard are streaked with grey, largely thanks to the mental stress, but that has not affected my overall appearance much. When I am once again able to stand properly and interact with others as I could in the past, I am sure I will be able to make friends, wherever I settle. At the moment, however, I am rather handicapped by the weight of stress and the aftermath of my little episode a while ago. It really has taken its toll on me, hence the need to lose my face.

Ah, yes. The face. You're probably wondering about

that, aren't you? Well, it was Dram's idea, you see. Coming here, I mean, coming here and losing myself. He did not put it as me losing a face though. No, in his mind it was rather that I would become somebody new, somebody with a *different* face.

"You can start afresh," he told me. "Nobody'll know you, nobody'll know what you've done or where you've been or who you were in the past. It's like a second life, buddy."

I remember looking at him and not being sure what to say. My neck was itching in the heat. I'd always itched and it had never got any better, no matter how many years I'd spent sweating my skin off in that sticky climate. I had a near-permanent rash down the back of my neck and on my legs. Horrid really. Why I stayed so long in that dripping jungle, I have no idea.

Ten years of sweat and mosquitoes and vile skin rashes and long, drowsy, pointless days in the bar and all the mistakes and regrets and blood and pain and now Dram was telling me I could be born again without all of it, could just leave it all behind and forget it, like it had never happened and wear a new face that people could meet for the first time. But he did not get it, because a man cannot exchange his face for a new one. This face is who you are too, not just what is beneath the surface, no matter what people may tell you. And once you turn away from that face, once you try to wear another, it is not a face any more; It is a mask and nothing more.

That is why I now have no face. I couldn't disagree with his reasons for encouraging my return to England, not at that time; Hell, at that time I could barely speak, so was in no position to argue. Besides, I owed him as much as he owed me and there was no reason to push the matter. Therefore, I left; Packed my bag and left everything behind, including my face. Dram had said at the time that perhaps it could just be for a while, but I guess he was being nice. I don't know.

I borrow Darren's computer in the bar to send an email with my contact details to Dram before I head out for breakfast. I am not certain he will ever reply, but I know I should do it anyway. After that I grab a scotch egg and a coffee in a cafe down the road and look over a map of the area.

Beyond making it this far, I did not really have any kind of plan for what to do in Oxfordshire. In all honesty, I do not know what to do with the rest of my life. This is supposed to be a new beginning, but without any real goal or purpose, it is hard to move forwards. While at the cafe I decide that the future can wait. I should settle myself back in slowly; There is no great hurry to do anything, and I need time to get my strength back.

Looking at the map, I pick a system of public footpaths that lead out through the countryside to some of the smaller settlements in the area and determine to visit one today. There is little that can compare, for its capacity to relax the mind and allow calm contemplation, to a good, long walk in the country. I'm sure you agree.

Leaving the cafe, I slowly make my way down the small, quiet high street. I walk carefully, but with renewed energy. I pull up my shoulders and try to adopt something of my former posture, and by god it feels good! I can hardly be said to stride, but I have not felt this energetic in a month.

This fact alone dispels the last of my anxiety about my situation.

The village really is quite beautiful, at least in the centre. Many of the houses have clearly stood for a long time, combinations of mortar and roughly-hewn stone. I run my fingers along the surface of the walls as I pass, tracing cracks and furrows beneath the tips as one might trace the grain in a wooden tabletop. I am quite alone and quite happy.

Beyond the westernmost block of cottages, the road narrows and becomes a surfaced bridleway, leading off into the fields on the outskirts of the village. The way runs between high banks of hawthorn and nettles and seems almost entirely devoid of traffic. Occasionally a cyclist will pass and once I encounter and exchange greetings with an elderly lady and her three labradors, but otherwise my slow progress is uninterrupted by the rest of the world.

After roughly a mile, a stile marks the path from the bridleway into the fields themselves. Even given my current physical misfortunes, I find the difficulty with which I cross the low wooden barrier depressing. Have I aged so much since last I walked out in rural England? As a child I would have leaped the stile in a flash and surely even ten years ago I would have moved more easily than this. My legs feel heavy and the soles of my walking shoes clip the beams in a way that aggravates me more than anything else. I feel like an old man and am again thankful for being alone.

The experience almost makes me give up on the walk entirely. I sit down on the stile and gaze out across the fields of golden wheat swaying lazily in the breeze. They spread out in front of me in all directions, climbing and falling with the topography of the landscape, interrupted only by dividing hedges, the occasional lone tree or a dark copse. My intended walk is to take me down the gentle slope of the valley, away from the woods at the crest of the hills. I can see the probable destination in the distance, a cluster of small houses and a church, partially obscured by trees and bushes.

Overhead a bird calls and I look up. I feel I should know more about the wildlife here, but either I have forgotten or never knew at all. By my side there is a plant, the name of which I *know* I knew when I was young. It is so common; A long green stalk separating into smaller, splayed sub-stalks, topped by small, delicate white flowers of five or six petals. I have seen it a million times in my life and once I knew its name. It makes me rather sad.

The idea of losing knowledge has been haunting me for a while, actually. For the past few years I have been growing increasingly worried that my mind is failing me. Once I even consulted a doctor on the matter, but he seemed unconcerned, blaming stress for distracting me, rather than the issue being a fact-haemorrhaging brain. Regardless, I really do feel I am becoming dumber. This upsets me more than it might many others, firstly because I have the intelligence to realise it, and secondly because I once had a fine mind, capable, focused, clear and with a seemingly-limitless capacity for information. Does everybody go through this at some point? If you are right now, try to take comfort in knowing you are not alone.

I slowly pull myself to my feet. It would be so easy for me to give up and head back to the inn, but I am better than that. Drawing a deep breath of the fresh country air, I smile a little to myself and begin to make my way across the field.

Beyond the footpath cut through the fields of corn, the pathway comes out onto a narrow road, eventually winding up past some farm buildings atop a nearby hill. I make my way past these without seeing a soul. Beyond the buildings, the footpath passes through a short section of undergrowth and I slow even more to lower my head enough to make it to the other side – but it is worth it.

Below me on the right side, the whole valley opens up and stretches to hills in the distance. To my left lies a dense expanse of conifers. Between the two runs a grassy ridge that slowly descends into the valley. In the sky high above, the bird I saw earlier tracks my progress – my private watchman. He is barely moving, riding the air currents and hanging like a harrier jump jet, gazing down at me. I touch my forehead in recognition, nod slightly and start down the ridge into the farmland below.

The sun is bright now, the land bathed almost entirely in warm light. Only here and there is it broken, where the shadows of clouds lazily slide across the landscape.

Otherwise all is warm and comforting and summery. That smell of sunshine hits my nose again as it floats on a barely perceptible breeze. I inhale it deeply and, still making my way down the ridge, I close my eyes for a while. The humming of insects weaves in and out of the rustling of grasses and leaves.

At the foot of the hill I stop and sit down in the tall grasses beside a field of corn. I pull off my sweater and ball it up into a cushion for my head, then lay back and listen. It is so peaceful here, no traffic or voices. Just the gentle sound of the grass shifting and insects passing. High above, my watchman hangs and more clouds make their way across the blue sky and my field of vision. Were I to stand on those clouds, I could reach out and touch the sky, dipping my fingers in cool blue and climbing away from the earth. And here there are gaps between them, gaps through which somebody might climb. For months the grey wall of clouds has covered everything, but here I am with crawling space and peace and breeze and insects and grass and the smell of the sun in my nostrils and its warmth on my body.

Cow parsley.

I smile a little and close my eyes.

Simulacrum

There comes from the base of my spine a deep grinding, whirring sound, like great, rusty gears twisting into motion together. The sound grows and dies with mechanical regularity; Grows and dies with the pain in my body on the hard wood of my bed. Thick brown sunlight hangs heavy in the air like noxious gas, burning through the small, barred window at the end of the tomb. Flies crawl across my face and bathe in the pungent sweat drying on my head. I breathe in slowly but there is no fresh air, just the stale stench from my own tongue and throat. The grinding, crashing sounds of metal continue.

I slowly turn my head to one side and look across at the opening at the side of the tomb. The cover is bolted shut from the outside and only a few slivers of light come through the gaps in the metal grating. Barely any air is coming through from there, even less than from the window at the end. Though gusts of breeze do come through, exposed by the layers of dirt and dust they pick up and blow inside, the air is thick and hot, and the wind cools nothing.

Beyond the grating comes the grinding sound of machinery, and something else. Screams – or are they barks? – come through the gaps. There is pain in them; Pain and vicious intent, but also something that sounds like language. The screeching is answered as well, answered with more squawks and screams.

Eeeeeyyyyyaaaaaaaagggggggg!

Eeeeeeeeyyyyyaaagg!

I listen in horror as the conversation continues, horror at the sounds and at the realisation that they are coming closer.

I stare, wide-eyed, at the window, then back at the grating; Back and forth, again and again, as the screams draw ever nearer. My body is immobile, both through agonising pain and the constricted confines of my prison. Try as I might to move, to get myself away from the terrifying, inhuman screeching, but I cannot. I can do nothing but stare in absolute mortification as a dark shape blocks the light beyond the grating and a final, deafening, blood-curdling shriek roars into the tomb.

As I open my eyes, the sky is red. Blood red. There is not a sound, not even of the wind, which has fallen still. The silence is almost deafening; The pumping of blood through my head is all I can hear. In the crimson sky above there are clouds, black as obsidian and the fields and hillsides around me are the same.

I look around, trying to get my bearings and that is when I see it. A human figure stands on the crest of the hill, a silhouette as black as the landscape, as if sprouting from the earth itself. It does not move, it does not make a sound. I stare at it, a growing feeling of terror in my belly. Ever so slowly, its head is tilting backwards. Just as slowly, it is raising its arms outwards from its sides and I can hear the screams again. The noise rises and rises, joined by other voices howling and screeching. I notice more of the figures now, some closer, others further away, all as black as pitch.

The screaming is becoming unbearable. Rage is turning to agony and terror and more and more of the voices are joining the chorus. The sounds coalesce into one massive drone, rumbling through the fields and hills, shaking the trees and loosening the hold of their roots in the soil. It is one ceaseless throbbing. I turn to find somewhere to run, but they are all around me now, some close enough that I can begin to make out features on their faces, and what I see pushes my mind over the edge.

I wake beneath an ear-splitting roar and a colossal shadow, gazing up into the silhouette of a vast, black bird. The grass shakes around my head and I stare, transfixed, at the gargantuan form of the C-17 as it sails overhead. I follow it with my eyes as it passes and sit up to watch it disappear behind a forest on the hills ahead.

I am completely alone in the fields. There are no manic screams or twisting shapes. There is only the smell of sunshine and the wind in the grass that sways around me.

Drawing a deep breath, I pull myself to my feet and look across towards the point in the trees where the C-17 disappeared. Undoubtedly it was on its way to RAF Brize Norton; The planes pass regularly over the village and fields.

Yet this one was different and I shudder at the thought.

I have been living in the village for a month now, renting the attic room at the far end of the building that once housed the stables at the Eagle. Darren had been wondering what to do with it and agreed to a discount on the rent in exchange for me doing some refurbishment.

I rather enjoyed the experience, actually. The feeling of building my own home – after a fashion, at least – made for good therapy and a good way to settle into the area. I may only be renting, but by repapering the walls, getting in a bed and installing other bits and bobs, I have allowed myself to feel less of a transient.

The work has also enabled me to get to know people in the local community a little better. Jim at the unfortunately monikered *Isis DIY* – named for our stretch of Old Father Thames, obviously, not for a bunch of backward psychotics – has become a regular collaborator on fitting the shelves and other pieces of furniture for the room, while Mrs Whitby, a darling, warm-hearted lady of advanced years, has been invaluable as an advisor on interior decoration.

After the incident with the C-17 and the unsettling and

unnervingly personal dream that preceded it, I decide to abandon my walk to South Leigh and return to the village to see Mrs Whitby about a vase she had recommended me. I suspect she has an ulterior motive in wanting to see me, but I am quite happy for the distraction at the moment and mind not a jot if she attempts to secure my services for some local project or other.

Mrs Whitby's small shop lies in the heart of the village, just up the main street from St Paul's church, tucked into the low-ceiled confines of a row of converted alms houses that now make up a small, but very convenient, shopping parade. *Isis DIY* inhabits the same row of buildings, along with a post office, sandwich shop and a *very* well-stocked off licence, the *Village Cellars* – run by Mrs Whitby's son-in-law, John.

I stop in at *Snacks* to pick up one of Jocelyn's excellent Cornish Pasties, then make my way into Mrs Whitby's place next door. The door opens with its customary creak and tinkle of chimes, onto the lady's private world of antiquities and parochial bric-a-brac.

Entering this shop is always like stepping back in time,

or at least that is how I feel. In truth it is, like many such places, an elaborately constructed and protected simulacrum of English rural life. Through intricately patterned net curtains, eternally golden light streams into the dim interior, seemingly keeping time in the shop forever captured in an early summer evening. Across the low, ancient ceiling with its thick oak beams and cream-coloured plaster hang bunches of dried flowers – lavender, mostly – that fill the air with a fragrance wonderfully conducive to dozing off for an hour or two. Indeed, I have found myself waking up in Mrs Whitby's easy chair on several occasions, a half-finished and cool cup of tea beside me on the table.

The shop's wares are displayed on shelves, cupboards and tables around the interior in a manner that at first can seem quite random, but there is a strange kind of art to Mrs Whitby's system of arrangement. The shop feels full, but never crowded; It is busy, but never cluttered. One never has to step around items to get to another part of the shop, and while continued exploration frequently reveals new discoveries, nothing can really be described as being hidden or obscured. No, this is a peaceful, self-contained world, the creator of which oversees it with the utmost care and attention to detail. I like it here.

Another remarkable feature of the shop is how quiet it is inside. The parade of alms houses sits right on the main road – not a heaving traffic artery, I'll grant you, but busy enough – yet once safely inside Mrs Whitby's fiefdom, one is enveloped in absolute peace and quiet. I once thought of asking her if she had installed soundproofing, yet realised that she would probably baulk at the suggestion of something so insidious and modern having intruded on her inner sanctum.

Today it seems even quieter than ever when I arrive. The air is warm and thick, the vaguest hints of aromatic dust drifting from the flowers above and the golden light casting its glow across everything. Mrs Whitby is not around, but that is normal, so I seat myself in her easy chair, pick up a used plate from the table beside me and begin to eat my pasty.

After a while, the sound of goods being shifted in the loft indicates Mrs Whitby's whereabouts and I wait for her to poke her head down through the open hatch near the passageway to the back room. It is these regular drawn out periods of waiting that have often led to my drifting off to sleep in this seat before, but today I want to avoid slipping back into the world of Dream as much as possible. It is no longer a happy place for me to be.

"Mrs Whitby!" I call out. "It's me!"

A muffled voice cheerfully calls back.

"Hello, dear! I'll be down soon. Make yourself comfortable."

"Can I make myself a cup of coffee?" I ask, knowing the answer as I speak.

"Tea or nought!" she calls back. "You must know that by now. Get yourself an Earl Grey."

I make my excuses – tea is not going to give me the kick I need today – and pop next door to grab a takeaway espresso from *Snacks*. By the time I return, Mrs Whitby has descended and is busy dusting off an old leather suitcase.

"I can't get used to coffee," she mumbles, "no matter how much I try. People used to laugh at me when all the other young folk were going to coffee shops and socialising, but I had to make do with church dances. Didn't do me any harm, mind! Met my Reginald at one of those and *he* didn't have much time for coffee either."

I listen and smile. There is something quite wonderful about Mrs Whitby's resolute old-fashioned approach to life. I can imagine her dressed up in her Sunday dress and bypassing the coffee shops and other haunts for young folk, heading straight through for a cup of tea with her mother and the vicar, hoping for good, wholesome Reginald to pop his head through the door.

This, perhaps, is as much a romantic fantasy as the shop itself, one I am equally guilty of perpetuating. Doubtless, like all young things, she was a darn sight more energetic and daring than she likes to admit today. Similarly, Dear Departed Reg cannot have been quite the simple tea-supping choirboy she likes to portray in her wistful remembrances. Doubtless he was a fine gentleman, but to hear her speak of their courtship you have to wonder how they ever wound up producing offspring.

Yet it is a harmless fantasy, and certainly not all fantasy at that. There *is* truth in the world she describes, I am sure of it. And who can begrudge anybody their sustaining an outdated and quaint lifestyle when the real world has degenerated into such an appalling heap? Better to dream than to wake up nowadays – unless your dreams have become as bad as reality.

"You called me about the vase," I say, hoping to refocus the conversation.

"A-ha!" she cries in something approximating triumph. "Yes, it's a lovely little thing. Let me find it."

She heads into the back room and after a swift rummage, returns carrying a slim, blue china vase. Then she seats herself in a deep embroidered arm chair, takes a sip of tea and presents me with the piece.

"There we go," she says, beaming proudly. "Isn't it beautiful?"

It *is* beautiful. The level of intricacy shown in the carving and patterning indicate a work crafted with great care and the glazing is perfectly balanced in terms of depth, extent and hue. I find Mrs Whitby's ability to source and acquire such fine pieces of work consistently amazing. She has an almost supernatural knack for chasing down the right pieces and ignoring those better left untouched. This vase is a particularly fine example and I am surprised when she asks only fifteen pounds for it.

"No, Mrs Whitby!" I half cry and half laugh. "This is a *beautiful* piece of work. You can't have paid so little for it yourself, can you?"

She winks cheekily and grins.

"It *is* lovely, isn't it?" she beams.

"It is, and I insist you not part with it for less than forty pounds."

"Call it thirty and we'll be done," Mrs Whitby says in her most commanding tone, the one which always dissuades one from responding in the negative. I smile and pull my wallet from my pocket, handing over three crisp tenners and helping her wrap the vase in crepe paper.

"Now, Mrs Whitby," I say, "was this vase the only reason you asked me to pop by?"

Another cheeky grin and she nods at the easy chair, seating herself on a rattan stool and sipping at her cup of tea.

"There's no hiding things from you, is there?" she says cheerfully. "I confess I *do* have something to ask of you, if you don't mind."

"Not at all," I say. "You know I'm largely unoccupied these days. What can I do to be of service?"

"The village carnival is coming up in a month, you know?"

I nod and smile again.

"Well, some of the WI ladies were hoping to get together a float in honour of Mr Churchill, this being a sort of anniversary, after all. We were wondering if we could enlist your services, being skilled and handy and all, in putting it all together."

"Of course, Mrs Whitby," I say. "I would be delighted and honoured!"

"Now, dear," she says, "there's no need to go overboard. It'd just be a small thing."

"No, really," I insist. "I'm really happy to help. I've been looking for a way to get involved in the carnival, beyond helping Darren out at the Eagle. This is perfect, and a tribute to Sir Winston is right up my alley as well."

It is agreed that I should meet the ladies of the village WI some time next week to discuss their ideas and requirements and I leave – new vase in hand – to head home for a while. I am still somewhat drained after my experience in the fields and fancy a nap before dinner.

I arrive back at the Eagle to find Darren taking delivery of a large order of bunting. He's getting things in early for the carnival so we can get started with preparations in the next week or two. The event will be an important one for him in particular, as this is his first year running the pub and he is keen to turn it into a community establishment as well as a hangout for the regulars.

'Hoi!' he calls as I walk in, waving at me. "Can y'give us a hand with all this when y'get a moment?"

"Sure, I'll just drop my things in my room and be back," I reply and turn to go.

"Oh," he says suddenly, as if remembering something. "Y'had a phone call. I took the number down on the pad by the phone."

I thank him and pick up the pad.

The call was from Dram.

Worship

I wake to the sound of rain hitting the window and the wheels of a bus pushing through the water on the road outside the pub. The room is dark, but my clock tells me that is due to the rain, not the time. The temperature has dropped as well; Must be around eighteen degrees, in contrast to the balmy twenty-three it has been averaging recently.

It takes time to get out of bed. I feel heavy again, have done ever since Dram's call – a call I have yet to answer. I am not as slow as I was on my return to the UK, but I have certainly regressed. It is harder now to motivate myself to get involved with Darren and the others in the village and I hate that. I know I should be up and about, working this out of my system, but it is just so difficult to do.

I pull myself to the mirror and gaze into the sad looking eyes before me. I look older; Older than before and older than my years. This is not healthy. I was very healthy at one time, but that time seems long ago. Perhaps today will help; I certainly hope the doctors can do something. Of course, the main purpose of this appointment is for me to help them, but in the process we all hope I can take some benefits as well. It is worth a try and it is not like I have much else to be getting on with until Mrs Whitby's project gets underway.

I stop by to see Darren in the bar before I head out. I feel bad for avoiding him for the past few days and I know he has been worried about me. I find him doing his accounts by the window and for a few moments he does not even notice I am there. I wait for him to glance up and am pleased to see him smile when he does.

"Whatcha!" he says loudly.

"How's it going?" I ask, trying to sound as normal as possible.

"Pretty good," he replies. "Reckon we can start getting things set up in the next week or two. Looking forward to it!"

"Me too," I say, grinning in what I hope is a convincing way.

"Glad to hear it," he says, smiling more widely. "I was getting a bit worried when y'disappeared for a few days. Y'alright?"

"Yeah, sorry. A lot on my mind."

"You need a project," he says with a little smile. "S'perfect for taking y'mind off things. Ah, speaking of which, can y'pick up some packs of wine glasses at Wilkos for us?"

I agree and head out to catch the bus into town. The rain is not letting up and the village streets are bathed in grey. I wait by the church, shivering pleasantly beneath my umbrella and watching cars pass by. When the bus finally arrives I make my way to the front seat at the top and curl up against the window.

Many people loathe this British rain and even Dram had whinged about it, despite simultaneously trying to persuade me to return, but I love it. Certainly, it is trying when one needs to get somewhere or do something and I would not want it to rain on a barbecue or the carnival day or anything, but there can be little in the field of human experience to compare with sitting atop a double-decker, wrapped up in a warm sweater, watching the rain fall in the streets outside.

I listen to the sound of vehicles pushing through the water on the roads, that lovely swishing sound that rises and falls as they pass. Sometimes I wear headphones for my journeys to town; It's so busy and crowded on some days that I like to lose myself in some flowing soundscape or other. But today I just enjoy hearing the rain fall and watching the green trees and sodden fields pass until we roll into George Street in the middle of Oxford and disembark.

Oxford in the rain is a sight to behold, at least in my opinion, and one I urge you to endeavour to experience if you have not yet had the chance. I huddle beneath my umbrella in a doorway to the Covered Market, watching the streams of water run down the glorious Headington limestone of the grand old buildings out in the High Street. There is *that* colour that I can associate with nowhere but here and in the gloom of this wet day, it takes on a deeper and even more refined character.

You may remember me telling you that I had not visited Oxford since I was a child, and that was true. Yet now I feel like I have been here all my life. There is something in these stones and paving slabs, in the ancient cut of the walls and the elaborate, yet tasteful, styling of the towers and spires; It is perhaps the weight of history, but – no – it is more than that. The stone *feels*, the walls watch and whisper. Run your fingers across the facades and you can hear them.

At first, I found it all very intimidating. It was so vast and so, so significant that I was shaken. I was so small and tiny and meaningless in the shadow of such might, such history and such worth. Yet as time passed I came to see things differently. The City is a benevolent grandparent, not a towering dictator. He welcomes me in and gives counsel, reassures and stabilises with His vast history and knowledge and understanding. More than that, He tells me that, far from being insignificant, I *do* have a purpose; Indeed, I have always had it. I just didn't know what it was at the time.

All these years, I have wondered at the purpose of my actions, for my striving – when I have striven – and for my struggle. In this glorious benefactor I have seen some sense of the truth, of the worth and meaning behind my trials and tribulations. I am no scholar. My history of academic achievement would impress nobody, but my understanding has grown with my experience of the world and it is that, along with the guiding hand of the Stone, that has started the process of self-awareness grinding and turning in my mind. I am no scholar, but for Him I have been a warrior. For the longest time, in spite of my blindness to the fact, I have been one of His most increasingly dedicated and loyal retainers.

It is at the end of the Turl that I find it. I am milling aimlessly, simply taking in the beauty of my surroundings and enjoying the aroma of a rainy day when, glancing down, I notice a scraping of college stone on the ground. It is unclear how it has come to be detached from the wall; Most likely somebody has knocked against it with a suitcase.

I peer from left to right and find myself alone. Reaching into my pocket I draw out the small vial I have been keeping for such a discovery. I picked it up at the pharmacy a few days ago and cleaned it out; It held perfume, which I obviously did not need. I have decided that I want a nice little display in my room. This is the first exhibit. Reaching down, I scoop the damp dust into the vial and give the top a wipe. Then I screw the lid tight and slip it inside my coat for safekeeping. Smiling a little smile to myself I make my way out of the lane and back onto the High Street.

I wait for a bus near that wise old guardian and perennial rendezvous fallback, Carfax Tower, as the rain hammers down in vast sheets around me. Water rushes in streams in the gutters down towards St Aldates and other people hurry from one shop awning to the next, huddling and snuggling beneath their own umbrellas. I cannot help but smile.

I board the bus and ride through the deluge and the city. Turning right at the foot of the hill that rises to Brookes University, the bus makes its way through rain-washed avenues of trees to the walls of Warneford Hospital, my destination.

Shivering with pleasure I make my way through the labyrinthine mass of buildings that make up the various departments and research laboratories of this vast university hospital, slipping under dripping archways and down tree-lined pathways awash with rain. At the far rear of the huge compound sits the building that houses the Department of Neurosciences and it is here that I meet with Dr Malgorzata Palacz, the researcher who seems so interested in the contents of my head.

I first got in contact with Dr Palacz after seeing an online advertisement requesting volunteer subjects for research into various forms of stress disorders. At the time, I was still recovering from my episode and thought it might be as helpful for me as for the Neurosciences team. Initially I just made a call for the sake of finding out what they were doing, but since Dram's phone call and my relapse I have come to appreciate that help might be required.

Dr Palacz is fascinated from the moment we begin talking. She has – coincidentally – been writing a paper on Post-Traumatic Stress Disorder and feels I fit the profile in some way. I feel like laughing at the idea until I realise that what I had been through recently might be considered a trauma. Dram's sides would split – or would they? Does he have more of an idea about this than I guess?

Dr Palacz explains the purpose and methodology of the project and gives me some preliminary questionnaires to browse through and answer while she contacts some people over at John Radcliffe Hospital to get an MRI scan approved. The questionnaires are fairly repetitive and she explains that they are all for different systems of diagnosing various conditions, so I guess all the crossover is natural. I fail to see how questions of motivation and energy relate to PTSD, but I am not a doctor, am I?

When we are done the doctor drives me over to JR Hospital for the scan. She attempts to make small talk and I attempt to respond with the usual kind of success and depth one expects from aimless chatter. I suppose I am worse at this kind of polite conversation than many others, as I simply cannot answer with honesty. The kind of questions one is asked always hover around topics about which I am understandably reticent. Today I probably get away with it, given my condition, but as I am attempting to settle into a new environment this is something that needs work.

The MRI scan is an odd experience. If you have never had one, what they do is slide you inside a giant plastic doughnut-cum-washing machine contraption and then blast you with noise for about an hour. I lie in the gloom inside the scanner, completely encased in plastic and metal, staring at the top of the tube only a few inches in front of my face. The grinding, honking, clicking noises start and I let my mind wander.

It wanders to Dram and what needs to be done there. It may turn out that he is doing nothing but calling to check on how I am, but I do not think it is helpful. Too many memories come flying back, memories better suppressed and hidden away in some dark recess of my mind. One missed call and I am back there again and it all gets too much. One message and I find myself in this scanner, listening to white noise and industrial clanking. I know I need to call him back, and perhaps when I do I should ask him not to call for a while. Maybe a few months. Or years.

At the same time, I have to get back to integrating myself in the village community. I am glad that Darren seems keen to get started on the prep for the carnival and I am looking forward to helping with the WI float. People are good there. They do not know me, of course, but they are good to me and it means a lot. I had forgotten what it was like to be treated well. So many years have passed and it has come as a shock now I'm back. I cannot say I expected it at all.

Maybe Dram was right and I certainly need to thank him for that. Maybe I can wear a new face here – no, maybe my face can simply be seen differently. Mrs Whitby and Jocelyn and Darren and Jim know nothing of my past. They see only who I am now and they like it. Their warmth has even begun to warm me inside, to let me calm myself, to let go of all the fear and anger of the past decade. Perhaps I can even wash away all the blood.

All at once, in that throbbing mechanised coffin, I am back in Jakarta – or was it Bangkok? Back there in Dram's sanctuary, that womb of sound and peace to which we always retreated when our work was done.

Deep, sonorous tones float across the interior of the Chamber of Silence. It must be understood that there is no contradiction in that fact. After all, this is a sanctuary dedicated to the silence of *light*. In its own way the droning artificial ocean only serves to intensify the isolation from the world beyond. Rumbling, throbbing, ever-changing and reforming, the sounds envelop we two men in the room, picking us up and transporting us.

Dram's project has always been a surprising one. Far from the act of destruction that I feared, this is a product of inspired creation. The contraption has many parts, but at the core of its system is a large, hollow stretch of bamboo trunk. The ends have been sawn off and carefully sanded to an almost polished shine. The bamboo cylinder lays on its side, suspended above the floor by long strands of twine which cradle it and keep it hanging free in space. These strands of twine are held up by a coat hanger that has been attached to the redundant light fitting in the ceiling.

In the upward-facing side of the cylinder, Dram has carefully cut an opening a few inches wide. This rectangular hole is strung with three electric guitar strings that are attached to either end of the cylinder; A guitar's tuning pegs and bridge having also been added to allow for setting the strings to different tones. The final part of the central instrument is a covering of thin material at one end, not unlike the skin of a drum. This has the dual effects of causing reverberation and channelling sound to the other end of the cylinder.

At the 'mouth' of the instrument sits a microphone, the cable of which runs down into a long chain of effects pedals, synthesiser modules and a mixing unit. All of this is hooked up to a set of speakers placed in opposite corners of the room.

All this has taken a long time to assemble, particularly in the dark of the Chamber of Silence, but its ultimate effect is overwhelming. Dram gently knocks against the side of the bamboo with a small mallet, sending deep reverberating sound waves through the microphone and into the complex of gadgets which is used to modulate the natural sounds of the instrument.

I sit in the darkness and listen as Dram slowly sets up undulating washes of sound, pouring across the room and back again. Occasionally he adds a new tone to the mix by affecting the strings on the top, emphasising one note or another, which is caught in the system of delay, echo and reverb units on the floor, feeding back into itself and eating its babies until it merges into the vast soundscape surrounding us.

Lost in this heaving ocean of sound, I feel a peace

unlike any other. At first I am unsure whether to listen directly or instead to try and focus on ideas inside my mind. Eventually I realise that it is better to allow my brain to empty itself entirely – or as fully as a brain so fragile and shaken can – and give myself over to the sound.

And all at once there is the surf, there are the trees, there is the pancake-flat image of Taketomi-jima; My toes curling in sand, sand shaped like stars; The shape of stars, stars, like dust; Stars on the beach and stars in the sea. All I have to do is reach down and touch.

My fingers run through the soft sand, stars falling between them as I lift them to my nostrils. The smell of the sea. The smell of stars. The warmth of the sun on my head.

The blue sea stretches on forever and there is no sound. God's tears, these islands; The fragments of a god's sorrow, raining down and forming land where they hit the vast blue. And ash walks the earth, ash of everything; Everything greater than it once was and one day will be again. This ash on the breeze; This ash *in* the breeze; This ash is the breeze and I am the breeze and here is nothing and everything all at once and there was just one moment like this when once I was free. Yet I was free only when there was no me and everything was me and I was nothing at all. An island song, riding the great winds, crossing the oceans, a friend with the birds and being the birds all at the same moment. An island song; A song of tears and wind and ash and stars and light and gods and sand and sea and blue and everything and nothing all at once.

And the cold water of the Arctic Ocean on my face, pulling back from nothingness and becoming truly awake and alive for a moment. Great plains of volcanic rock; Grass and moss, stretching to the horizon like the great blue of the sea. Here the song has become a roaring, raging, powerful wind; Gusts of melody and notes and those tears – now dry – pulling against me as I lean into them, eyes squeezed tightly closed. My friends are there too. I have friends then. They too let the wind and song carry them as it rips across the vast open spaces at the top of the world. There is nobody else, and only then can they become something. Only when surrounded by complete nothingness, by vast, swollen waves of wind and song, tearing across the grass and rock, swallowing us and making us everything all at once.

The church bell tolls and we wonder if it is a wedding. But no, not a bell like that at a wedding; That is a funeral bell, surely.

You wouldn't toll a bell like that at a wedding, would you?

And the bell tolls and gas bursts through the fissures of the orange earth in the deep plain beyond the mountains. The mountains, even further beyond the ocean of black rock of the caldera. And there at the end of the road we find the might of Dettifoss, its roaring power at one with the wind and the sand and the stars and the sea and the song and nothing and everything, and everything all at once. It falls and pounds and rips away into the rock and we fall with it; Fall like the gods and fall like the songs and fall like a million holy tears on vast blue seas.

A million miles from here.

A million miles from this hell.

A million miles from consciousness and the knowledge

of all the lies. A million miles from Man, who has tried to make Himself *something* and cannot hope to be nothing.

A million miles.

The scan ends and Dr Palacz thanks me for all my help. We set up the transfer of payment – an agreeable bonus, I must say – and agree to meet in a few weeks to discuss the results of the scan and identify anything that can be done to help. We part at the rainy bus stop and she catches her bus first. I stand in the gloom beneath my umbrella and watch the bus pull away. In spite of the ceaseless rain, I feel warmer now. Movement may make any road seem right, but it may just be that I am finally on the right road – a road out of the darkness.

The number ten bus pulls up and I board it, settling down for the ride back to the centre of town.

Brontide

I remember Darren's request for wine glasses about two minutes before the bus is set to pass the Knight's Plaza shopping centre where Wilkos is located. I alight to the same wall of rain, yet in the greater gloom of these surroundings it is less comforting, more oppressive. I had hoped to avoid this area altogether, but for Darren's sake – and for the sake of our growing sense of collaboration – I must brave it.

The Knight's Square shopping centre is one of those horrific concrete monstrosities that one can find stinking up any area of the UK in which investment has not been made for the past two decades. Stained, grey, Auschwitzian blocks make up the angular passage that leads into the centre itself, shops squeezed in the length of the tunnel like cells on a prison block. From the bus stop the first four businesses I can see through the veil of drizzle are betting shops, with a tanning salon sandwiched in the middle for good measure.

Gaunt, acned, pasty-faced youths – I hope for their sake they *are* still youths – smoke by the doorways, wearing masks of utter contempt for passers-by. This is what happens in mid-sized towns across the world; Too big to retain any sense of tradition, community or shared culture, too small to have anything to do or anything going on.

Taking a deep breath I make my way across the street to the cracked cement walkway leading beneath the rectangular concrete block that acts as a kind of archway. The ground is a mass of cigarette butts and chewing gum long since trodden in and hardened. A truly Dante-esque experience, I feel my spirit evaporating with every heavy step.

How can it have come to this? In ten long years living in the developing world I cannot recall having seen such a desolate, despairing landscape. Perhaps that was because there was hope there – a sense that things were improving and might continue to improve for some time. Is this what it looks like when hope dies? A dessicated wasteland of motivation and dreams and purpose and nothing more.

Few faces I see as I descend into the centre give any

indication of being exceptions. Skeletal, strained men worn away through years of fags and lager stalk through the scene, eyes popping out of their heads and carrier bags full of Fosters cans dangling from their hands; Women with pushchairs and tracksuit bottoms, hair stretched back into severe ponytails, huddle together to shelter from the rain, expressions fevered and intense as they scribble away at lottery scratch cards; Vast men and women undulate through the centre's main doors like rolling oceans of flesh, not one of them able to smile; Angry-looking, scarred skinheads stare fixedly ahead at some point in the distance as they stride aggressively into the rain; Gaggles of women in hijab frown and glare suspiciously from the doors as they wait to see if the clouds will pass.

Inside the main hall things are too dim for this kind of centre, but are a little better than the vision of Hell outside. The screams of children echo along the blank walls, mixing with the standard shop soundtrack of thumping House, bland indie and vapid RnB, but somehow people do not look quite so wasted. It is as if some ever-weakening forcefield holds the decay at bay. It feels like *Dawn of the Dead*.

The staff in Wilkos are nice though. One woman in particular exhibits the kind of intense enthusiasm for helping customers that suggests ingestion of narcotics. She damn near foams at the mouth – in a thoroughly friendly and warm way – as she directs me to the glassware section at the rear of the store, making rapid-fire chitchat and beaming the whole way through. The rest of the staff must find her extremely annoying as, far from giving poor service as they are, they can hardly compare. Her name is Joan and she makes my trip into the Inferno well worthwhile.

Weighed down with bags full of packs of ultra-cheap wine glasses for the pub I waddle back to the front of the centre and out of the entryway. Near the top of the passage I walk slap bang into the middle of an abusive exchange between two groups of youths. The female group is wandering past on the opposite side of the road while the collection of slouching males lean against the wall of one of the betting shops, hurling abuse across the street.

"Oi! What you lookin' at eh?" an exceptionally spotty and pale boy screams, to be answered in similarly charming fashion by what I take to be the lead girl.

"Go fuck y'self, yer wanker!"

"What? You love it!"

And so on.

I slide past the group, who are getting a remarkably small amount of attention from other shoppers; One has to assume this kind of thing happens all the time. There is something unsettling about it though, as if it could spill over into violence, and not necessarily just between the two groups. While the two main abusers are shouting at each other, other members of the groups are eyeing passers-by, seemingly without embarrassment, checking for any objections.

I try my best to avoid eye contact, but cannot help getting the attention of one of the boys.

"Fuck you lookin' at?!" he shouts at me and I stop moving, glancing around as if I do not realise he is talking to me. He starts stalking over and the boys turn their attention from the girls to me.

"Yeah, you, old boy!" the oik shouts as he draws closer. Some of the other boys add jeers of their own and, depressingly, so do some of the girls. It is as if I have interrupted some territorial dispute or mating ritual – the second being more likely – and messed up all the rites. Any previous animosity between the groups has disappeared and, given that this probably *is* an act they perform frequently, it has been redirected at this foolish interloper.

The boy stops a few metres from me, his intensely forced aggression pumping from every pore in his skin. He breathes deeply through his mouth and stares bug-eyed at me as I try to remain calm. A few other shoppers have half stopped to watch, but otherwise we are alone.

"What you lookin' at?" the boy asks again.

I am trying very hard to slow my mind down and decide how to reply without exacerbating the situation, but my current condition makes it harder.

"Nothing," I eventually mutter.

"What?" the boy says. "Speak up!"

He takes another step towards me, deliberately giving a strange aggressive shrug motion, as if to threaten me. My hand instinctively slips into one of the shopping bags and curls around the neck of one of the glasses. All of a sudden I feel calm and peaceful again, the old familiar routine comforting in its certainty. The boy can see something change in my expression and he hesitates for the briefest moment, a flicker of caution on his face. We stand looking at each other for what feels like an eternity. All other sounds around us have gone, but for the wind and the patter of rain as it hits the ground around us.

"Leave it, Den," the leader of the boys shouts over. "He ain't worth it!"

Another slight flicker crosses the face of the one called Den, something that might be relief, and he turns and stalks back to his friends with a "Watch y'fuckin' self".

He'll never know how close he came.

I gaze out across the rain-washed countryside as the bus carries me home and find myself full of conflicting emotions. The knowledge of how close we came to violence horrifies me, while the fact that my readiness gave me such comfort leaves me nothing but confused. The landscape beyond the window reassures me with its gentle hills and stone walls, and yet now it seems less permanent;

Threatened, vulnerable, naïve. Mrs Whitby's quaint fantasy of a life suddenly seems more the rule than the exception. How little it would take for the floodgates to crack and drown everyone and everything.

Magpie

I sit in silence on my bed, looking across at the shrine on the table before me. On the lined wooden top sit the first few items of worship: The vial of dust, a postcard showing Radcliffe Square and a small collection of leaves gathered from the abbey grounds to the south of the Eagle. I have carefully arranged them in what I consider to be an aesthetically-pleasing manner. The vial and postcard sit side by side; The leaves are arranged around behind and to the sides of them, a few placed in front like a carpet before a throne on which a very small man might engage in genuflection and prostration.

The fear and anger of my visit to town is gone. The process of arranging the items on the table has calmed me and now I sit in peace as the daylight fades beyond the window. My mind feels clearer and serene. I trace the edges of the leaves with my eyes, taking in the curves, the small tears and pits created by insects and the veins that run through them. I do this until I can no longer see them clearly and then lie down and close my eyes.

The dreams do not come.

Project

There is a thin mist hanging low over the village this morning, the rooftops shrouded and sleepy. The view from the skylight set into the sloped ceiling of my bathroom is always quite wonderful and today it is better than ever. There is barely a sound from outside; A few birds chatter in the trees, somebody's footsteps clop down the road; Leaves move gently in the breeze. The air smells fresh and crisp, not cold, but alive and full of possibilities.

I wash and descend the stairs to the bar, where Darren is already laying out the mass of bunting, signs and wooden posts for the day ahead. The bar itself is covered with things and there is considerable overflow on the tables and floor.

"Well, now," he beams at me as I walk in. "Are y'ready for an honest day's work?"

"Just point me in the direction," I reply, grabbing a hammer and a small pack of nails from the bar.

"Woah, woah, easy now," he laughs, palms spread apart, face down. "I didn't mean *that* fast! First things first an' all that, an' I reckon first thing's a coffee, eh?"

"Good idea," I agree. "Want me to make them?"

"Mine as black as night, if you please!"

I get the coffee machine whirring and gurgling while Darren does the final inventory check. We have a good amount of work to do today and he is hoping we can get the lion's share of it done before he opens the bar at one o'clock. I have offered to put up the bunting first, while he hangs the signs and other necessaries around the inn. We will work together to put up the elaborate collection of archways and other frameworks which Darren hopes will make the Eagle's contribution to the carnival just a little bit special.

The machine does its work and the smell of rich Kenyan Arabica, bitterness and spice in perfect balance, fills the bar area, causing both of us to pause for a moment and slip into blissful reverie. Truly there is nothing like the feeling of a project lying before you and experiencing no pressure, only pleasure at the thought. We both glance across at each other and cannot help but grin big, stupid grins. We drink our coffee while going over the plans for the morning and making sure we have all the things we will need individually. Once finished, we part; Darren heads outside with a pile of signs under one arm while I get up on a step ladder and start pinning the bunting up around the bar with tacks.

Darren has picked out multinational bunting, which I like better than the straight Union Jack stuff, as it is more colourful. It also avoids the chance of winding up with those aggravating Union Jacks that have the diagonal red lines dead centre, rather than the correct pinwheeling on the genuine article. While I work I amuse myself by trying to name all the countries represented on the string of flags and am impressed by the range on display. Somehow I would not have imagined British bunting producers choosing Kyrgyzstan and Swaziland, but clearly I underestimate them.

The work is good, so good that I do not even recall my dreams until later. The dreams of shapes and prison cells and blood red skies come far less frequently now, although ever since my experience with the townie youths they have intensified when they do. Now the screams are closer and closer every time, black eye sockets peering through the windows at me. The walls of the cell seem to be squeezing closer and closer together as well. I have woken to find myself unable to breathe, drenched in sweat, my head spinning with dizziness. Yet then I always look to the shrine and feel calmness returning. At any rate, as I say, they come less frequently.

I still have not called Dram back and – much like many other parts of life at the moment – it is filling me with conflicting feelings. On the one hand I have found myself thinking less and less about him and the life I left back in the tropics. More and more days pass before I pause to think about it. At the same time, feeling so comfortable with leaving everything behind, forgetting aspects of that life so easily, well, it all makes me feel like a traitor.

He sent me away, I can argue with myself at times, but I know that is only part of the story. He did it as much for me as for himself. After that final collapse, the unthinkable that snapped my brain, neither of us would have benefited from my remaining. I should thank him, and I do – at least in my own mind. Yet I cannot pick up the phone to let him know and it is *that* which is shaking my confidence. Because I know what memories his voice will bring back and I know what that will do to this little life I am building for myself. It will crack the face I am trying to wear and then there will be only two options, equally appalling; I could live without a face, or I could take the old one back and pull it on, blood and all.

I do not want that.

I like it here, I really do. It is strange to say it, but it is good to be back among human beings once again. For all the fragility and artifice in this life, it is a life I want to live and these are people with whom I want to live it. You should have seen the look on Mrs Whitby's face when she saw the early stages of the WI float being drawn up; Her eyes sparkled like a woman half her age and pride was bursting from her chest with every exclamation of excitement and pleasure. She was so proud to be part of this little village festival. It may sound utterly absurd and backward even to people of my generation, let alone the younger generations, but as I have said before, dreams and fantasies may often be the only sensible response to this craphouse of a world.

I can do this. I am certain that I have what it takes to hold all of this together and keep building it. I just need Dram to get the right message; I would not want to hurt him any more than I already have.

I finish with the bunting in the bar and head outside to the street to hang it along the inn's facade as well. The building looks so much better from the outside; Ancient dark beams running along the stone-built walls, thick thatch hanging down from the roof. It is a big place too, the old stables going around the side and creating a huge courtyard round the back that is perfect for this kind of event. Darren is planning a barbecue out there and wants to get some local bands in to perform. His enthusiasm is infectious and I happily forget my worries and spend the next half an hour banging tacks into the beams and hanging the bunting.

"Morning," a voice calls from below me. I turn and see Jim, a bag in his hand.

"Morning," I reply.

"Going well?"

"Yeah, we're having a lot of fun. I think we'll have most of the decorations done by lunch. How about you?"

"Yep, business is fantastic with folk building all these floats an' that. Just popping round to the Whitby place to drop in a few bits the WI lot need. Aren't you helping with that too?"

"Sure am," I reply, beaming. "Got all my fingers in pies this month!"

"Including the pie contest?" Jim shoots back, chortling at his own joke. I laugh too and admit that my baking skills might not be up to it.

"I've got some more nails for you chaps," Jim says. "Shall I leave them with you?"

"Sure," I reply. "Can you leave them on the bar?"

He nods and wishes me well before heading round back to see Darren. I finish up my work on the facade and return to the bar myself.

12:54pm.

Darren and I slouch behind the bar on stools, beads of sweat on our foreheads and pints of Otter Amber in our hands. We have not quite managed to get all the wooden construction done, but we can surely be proud of our level of achievement; The Eagle is going to look the business come carnival day.

Neither of us says much as we sit there. We are not weary, but revelling in the enveloping contentment that accompanies satisfying work. All told it must be this that is the greatest reward for our endeavours. We sit and watch the dust hang in the air, lit by the beams of golden light that now filter through the net curtains into the bar. That glorious scent of nuts and beer and wood floats around us and lulls us to drowsiness.

A knock comes at the door and Darren calls out that it is unlocked. A couple of the inn's regular patrons poke their heads inside and shuffle in to take their stools by the bar. Darren struggles to his feet and grabs a couple of pint glasses.

"Whatcha, gents. Pint of the usual?"

The man I know as Colin has a strained look on his face and does not smile when he speaks.

"Thanks, mate, but I need somethin' a bit stronger. Gimme a whisky."

"Same fer me," his friend says. I think his name is John, but I'm not sure.

Darren raises his eyebrows a little and reaches for a pair of tumblers and a bottle of Glenfiddich.

"Right you are," he says quietly. "Something up?"

"Jesus Christ!" Colin splutters. "Ain't y'eard the fuckin' news?"

Darren glances at me and I shrug. There is something unsettling about the men's faces. Darren turns back to them and shakes his head.

"Well turn it on! They're not showin' anythin' else!"

Darren picks up the remote, flips on the television and pulls out another two tumblers.

Wolves at the Door

Silence hangs across the pub like a thick grey pall of cloud. For all the people now here – at least eight of us altogether – there is barely any movement to disturb the heavy air. Yet for all its physical stasis, the room reverberates with raw emotion; Rage, horror, sorrow, shock.

Colin lays his head down on the bar, his third tumbler of Glenfiddich empty beside him, and exhales slowly. In the funereal atmosphere of the room, his breath sounds like a hurricane approaching, which may be exactly what is happening. John reaches over and rubs Colin's shoulder in an attempt to comfort him, but his face shows the same stricken sense of disbelief.

Darren stares at the wall, his face twitching at times and shifting from one expression to another; Shock, resignation, anger, sadness, then finally anger again before he mutters "Christ." He stands up and walks outside for a piss and the rest of us just look down at the floor for a moment, lost inside ourselves.

The news that Darren and I had managed to miss is that some militant bastard has turned up on a beach in Tunisia and machine-gunned families on holiday in the sun. Whole generations must have been wiped out as this piece of dog shit stalked across the sand, firing at random into parents, grandparents, kids, throwing bombs into hotels and blowing people apart. The news reporter on the telly could barely speak, the poor bugger.

What do you say?

All of a sudden it feels even more vulnerable to be here. This village, this land, this world. A storm of savagery is washing across the globe, a storm of blood and psychotic, backward idiocy. The bar is a feeble fortress in which to hide, but hiding is all we have energy for now.

"What d'you think they'll do?" John asks nobody in particular. "The government, I mean."

"Hope they find the bastard and kill him," Colin growls through his teeth.

Darren walks back in from the toilet and pours himself

another pint of Otter.

"Want one?" he asks the room. "It's on the house."

A few people nod, me included. I help Darren pour a few of the pints for the others and get my own at the same time. John thanks me for his and downs half of it in one go.

"Feels like it's so bloody easy for 'em now, don't it?" he says. "It's happening all over. All that in Paris and Denmark n'all."

"You know what it is?" I mutter. They look at me, a little surprised. I guess I have been quiet, wary of what I might say if I let my emotions get the better of me.

"It's they're feckin' loonies is what it is," Darren opines. There is much nodding of heads.

"I agree," I continue. "Bunch of psychotics living in a bloody fantasy world. But that's not the big problem, you know?"

"Well, what d'you think it is?" Colin asks, taking a sip of his pint.

"They think we're soft."

"*We* meaning?"

"Europe. All our liberal approach to things, all our

trying to understand our enemies and talk, all this human rights and solidarity protesting and - "

"You can't be wanting to ditch all that," Colin retorts, perhaps missing my point.

"No, no," I exclaim quickly. "Not at all! That is what we should be proud of. It's a good thing. Trust me, I've lived in places where it's nothing but hot air, or they don't even claim to give a shit. For all the problems we've got, it doesn't come close."

"So what do you mean, then?" John asks.

"How did we get to the point where we could worry about all that?" I reply. "We didn't get anywhere or build these societies by letting backward scum push us around, but either we've forgotten that or, at the very least, they *think* we've forgotten it."

"He's got a point," Darren says, having another sip of his beer.

"Too right," I say. "Somebody threatens you, somebody bombs your underground or shoots up a newspaper or cuts off heads, you don't waste time talking to the bastard; You stick a missile down his neck and remind his mates that you have balls to back up your ideology."

They look at me, John nodding thoughtfully, Colin grimacing but clearly thinking about what I've said. Darren raises his glass a bit, in a gesture of agreement. I smile at him a little, but I'm too into this train of thought now and cannot break it.

"I get y'point, mate," Colin says, "and I'm as upset as the next man about all this. But if we don't talk an' all that and don't try to be better then we're as bad as these bastards, aren't we?"

I ponder this a little, looking out the window at the golden sun in the street. Across the road Jim is clipping the hedge outside his house while his wife is filling up a bird feeder in the garden beyond. There is little sound now, just the twittering of birds outside the open inn door. I close my eyes for a moment, trying to hold that feeling and stop it slipping away. Then I open them and see Jim torn apart by a hail of bullets; His chest is ripped open as round after round flies through his body, his ribcage shattered, splitting apart in a shower of crimson gore; His eyes are blown out, his teeth splintered and falling to the floor as his body pirouettes and falls. The stream of shells flies through the hedge as easily as moving through air, Jim's wife caught in the storm; Her legs blown off at the knees, her screams frozen in time and she tumbling to the floor and the river of blood.

"Suppose you're right," I say.

"I guess," Colin agrees. "Can't just let people push you around though, even if you have ideals, I suppose."

"None of us would be sitting here if our ancestors had sat back and taken it, you know?" I say. "I believe in it all, don't get me wrong. I don't know, maybe I'm wrong. I hope I am, but, I don't know."

"I'm with you, mate," John says, raising his glass. Colin smiles a bit and nods at me, raising his glass as well. I respond in kind and lean back against the bar.

I respect Colin's opinion; The man has the right ideas in a sense, the ideas on which this society is supposed to stand. Perhaps I am speaking in a regressive way myself, but no matter what I say to him I refuse to believe I am wrong. It is becoming clearer and clearer to me that this is my role, always has been my role. I may not have known it in the past, not realised the true purpose of all my fighting; I may not have realised exactly for what and for whom I was dirtying my hands, but the truth was there all along, waiting for me to come to it in my own time and my own way. Who would ever have thought it would take the parochial surrounds of an Oxfordshire village to bring it all home to me?

Did Dram know? I doubt it. Dram may have wanted me gone as much for the storm that I had brought down on us both as for any concerns for my mental health or sense of self-worth. I had not messed up, at least in his eyes, but he had every right to suggest I leave. And once again it may have been exactly what I needed and just one more thing for which I have to thank the man.

I leave my spot behind the bar and wander to the door, pint in hand. The sun is bright in the old street; A warm wind ruffles my hair and carries the heat of the day across my skin. Jim waves at me from across the road and calls out to say he will be over for a pint in a little while. I raise my glass to him and give his wife a wave too. The two of them carry on with their work, lost in the moment and the light of the day.

Home Guard

I sip my beer and watch.

Satu

Blood and bone.

All I can see are blood and bone and the vast, cavernous mouths of the dead as they scream and scream, rupturing my eardrums with the sound. Their fingernails, long and ragged months after death, scratch along the skin of my legs as they reach through the barred windows of my cell; The cold touch more agonising than the ripping of flesh. The noise echoes and resounds within the narrow confines of the room.

There is no escape.

I am alone in the tunnel. Dram has left me behind and ventured further ahead. The stench of sewerage rises from the stream running between my legs. I adjust my feet slightly, trying to get a steadier foothold along the edge of the tunnel floor. A few metres in front of me, lit by the beam of my head torch, I can see the rotting corpse of a rat floating on the surface of the foul trickle of water. Its bloated form weeps as maggots push through its flesh to fall, sink and die in the filth that surrounds their macabre vessel.

Far ahead I can see a pinprick of light. It grows and dims at irregular intervals as Dram turns his torch one way and another. I crouch down as far as possible and watch as he scans the darkness for side tunnels. After a few moments he gives me the signal – three flashes – and I begin to edge my way silently along the foul interior of the drain.

I reach Dram's position at an intersection, three tunnels stretching off into the distance ahead and to the left and right. He is fiddling with our folded schematic of the sewer system. We have gone off the edge and he has to take it out of the protective plastic cover that hangs from his neck to reorganise it. I wait, shining my headlamp off into the inky blackness that surrounds us in every direction. The smell is worse here and I smear another glob of odour-masking gel under my nose, offering him some as well.

Dram is looking frustrated, although I avoid looking at him directly so my headlamp does not blind him while he is

Home Guard

checking the map. We have been crawling through these dank, stinking tunnels for a long time, far longer than anticipated and I am sure we have got lost. I say nothing, but the look on Dram's face shows that he is thinking the same.

"Where is this guy?" he mutters to himself. "I swear I've been following the map, mate."

"Bloody reeks down here though," I gag. "Reckon they just marked him down wrong?"

Dram says nothing and just keeps looking at the map, then down each passage in turn. Finally he looks back at me and grimaces, giving a small shrug of the shoulders.

A sudden distant clang resounds somewhere in the system of pipes and tunnels. We both freeze and stare at each other. I hold my breath and slowly close my eyes, straining my ears. The sound comes again, followed by clear footfalls. Dram points at his head torch and we kill the lights.

I strain my ears and can now clearly make out the footsteps of more than one person. There are most likely only two of them, but their being here is a complete surprise and most unsettling. As they draw closer, I can hear them

86

start to speak to each other. Clearly our being here will be as big a surprise to them. I listen to them, trying to make out what they are saying. The language sounds like Indonesian, I decide. Yes – it is. One of the men is asking the other where to go next, and then *"Dimana dia?"* - *Where is he?*

I tense up – they are here for the same reason we are. I wish I could speak to Dram to let him know, but I do not want them to hear us. I am wondering what to do when a cry comes from the next tunnel, very close now.

"Dia masih di sini!"

They've found him. I reach behind my back and slide the knife from its sheath. Quickly I shuffle forward, legs still splayed apart, trying to balance on the edges of the tunnel. One of the men hears and gasps. I slap Dram on the shoulder as I find him and snap on my headlamp again.

"Kamu siapa?" I shout, prompting another gasp from round the corner. "Kamu siapa?" I ask again – *Who are you?*

"Anda siapa?" one of the men responds in surprisingly polite language, perhaps uncertain of what tone to adopt until he knows who we are. I tense up my legs, flick the headlamp to a rapid-fire strobe and then throw myself

round the corner, angling my head so as to blind them as much as possible.

The next few moments slow to a crawl as I take everything in, processing every piece of information as it enters my head. The body of our target lies in the sewerage, his face caved in, yet moving – a writhing mass of maggots. Beside him stands one of the men, a stocky, muscular frame, fists clenched and eyes wide. The second, a lithe and athletic-looking man, stands further back in the tunnel. His hand is moving towards a knife attached to his belt.

My strobe light catches the first man the worst and he instinctively closes his eyes. I am on him in a second, my knife's razor-sharp blade tearing through the right side of his throat as I pass. I do not stop for a moment – he is done for, falling into the foul stream with blood already arcing from the wound in thick jets. The second man has his knife only halfway out as I come upon him, but my foot slips for a moment and as I pitch forward I know I am going in the water.

I hit the stream, the light from my headlamp flickering for a moment before it is smashed to pieces against the cement floor of the tunnel. In my horror I have only managed to close my mouth partially and thick liquid spills past my lips. And I swear to god there is a fucking turd against my tongue and I gag, retch and vomit in a moment, my lunch piling out into the sewer.

Through the tears bursting from my eyes as I vomit uncontrollably I see Dram fly past me down the tunnel, the beam from his headlamp shaking this way and that as he pursues the second man, who has turned tail and run back down the pipe. I pull myself out of the water and grab at the wall to try and keep myself steady as I gasp for air. But there is no air that is not full of the smell of shit and piss and vomit and raw effluent. Still I pull myself forwards, not wanting to lose the guiding lights from ahead if they turn a corner. I am desperate to move now, as much to find a way out of this vile system of pipes as to catch up to the men in front of me.

I pick up speed as the cramping in my stomach muscles eases up a little. I round a corner only a few moments behind Dram. The man is part way up a ladder and reaching for the hatch above, but Dram has hold of his leg and is stabbing at it with his knife. Blood is splashing down onto his face. He must have cut an artery in the leg. I run forward to help him and leap up to the ladder above him, but as I do so the man knocks the hatch open and screams out. He falls backwards past me into the tunnel, but I do not pay any more attention to him.

Above me I can hear the shouts and clattering and hell he has brought down on our heads.

Float

The women of the WI seem a fairly divided lot, considering the image Mrs Whitby painted of them when inviting me. A woman named Mrs Arnham, wearing a permanent scowl, is holding court and loudly decrying each and every suggestion for the design of the float. It would not really matter so much if she had an idea of her own, but she does not. Mrs Whitby is losing patience and repeatedly demands that Mrs Arnham refrain from embarrassing the WI in front of "our guest".

That's me.

A few of the ladies have brought sketched proposals for the project and I confess I can see why some of them have riled Mrs A. One staggeringly odd concept has a cardboard cut-out of Churchill atop a car, framed by giant rifles made of wood. This is swiftly cast aside as being rather negative, as well as stupid. Still, Mrs A's strident attitude is trying and I cannot help feeling that my time is being wasted here. The festival is not far off now and if they want something to parade, the ladies of the WI need to get their act together. Quickly.

Discussions are adjourned for a spot of tea and some cream cakes, along with standard issue chatter about bad backs, family gossip and whinging about each other. I mill around at the back of the hall and peer out at the rain clouds beyond the window. My own project is moving forward more agreeably than the WI float and the rain on the horizon will add another piece of the puzzle. I have put an old jam jar out on the steps below my room to catch some of the rain when it comes. That will be used for some grasses and daisies I have picked for the shrine.

Assembling and arranging the features on the table definitely has a therapeutic effect and I have felt calmer since starting it. Alongside the vial, the picture and the leaves I now have a postage stamp from the coronation year and a small collection of old coinage that I have placed in a pattern across the tabletop. I sit for a time every evening, taking it all in and slowing my breathing to help me relax. It is working; I feel more content again and the dreams – when they come – leave me less drained. Darren has noticed the change as well, commenting on it frequently as we work around the pub and get things ready.

I am glad he seems happy. He has been good to me and I owe him for it.

The meeting in the hall breaks up so people can go home and "consider things more carefully" (Mrs Arnham). Apologies are made for taking my time with little outcome and I smile them off as graciously as I can, promising to come again once plans are finalised. Then I make my way home as the rain starts to fall and sit for a time looking out of the window of my room, enjoying the sight of the drops as they make their way down the glass.

At four o'clock I collect my jar from the steps and put the grasses and daisies in the water. It sits nicely among the leaves to the rear of the display and I feel content as I lie back on the bed and watch the shadows of raindrops play across the scene until I nod off for an hour.

Once again, there are no dreams.

Comrade

It is raining in the woods, a little north of the village, where I find myself making plans invariably destined to generate controversy. A quiet pitter-patter sounds above as I shiver slightly beneath my umbrella. The rain has brought out the rich, earthy aroma of the woodland; Moss and fungi and damp tree bark, a whole world of insects and other creatures hidden away below.

Nestled below the boughs of some of the trees is another community of sorts. Four caravans and a rusty car sit immobile, dead leaves a carpet on each roof. To one side a small open grill smoulders, occasionally letting off steam as drops of rain fall onto it from the branches above.

Ned is about twenty-five by my reckoning. He has the pallid complexion symptomatic of an unbalanced diet and slight malnutrition, but his eyes are lively, his smile broad and his energy infectious. He sits with an equally malnourished dog – a boxer, predictably – and tickles it vigorously as it rolls about on the wet ground, panting frantically. I let him continue with this for a few moments, until he slumps back into the rusted garden chair beside the grill, sweat starting to bead on his brow.

"What was his name again?" I ask.

"Her name," he grins – I shrug in apology. "Princess," he sighs. I smirk a little, hoping he won't mind. He doesn't.

"Your choice," I ask, "or...?"

"Me mum's," he grimaces. "I wanted to call her Zelda, but we had to compromise, you know?" He grins again at this and I laugh.

Princess scrambles up off the wet leaves and scampers off into the undergrowth nearby after some prize or other. Ned yawns and stretches, leaning back in the chair, then prods at a sausage sizzling on the grill with a poker.

"I don't know, mate," he says after a long pause. "I don't get the feeling anybody's gonna like it." He glances up at me with a grimace on his face.

I look back up at the trees and breathe in. I have asked Ned and his family if they would like to help out with the barbecue at the Eagle next weekend. Darren has been looking for extra hands but, between the floats and the stalls and the music and the events there are precious few people left unoccupied to keep the fires burning and the sausages on the go. I have turned to Ned not just because I see him grilling away every time I walk up this way, but because I believe in having his family a part of things.

Ned, his mum and his younger brother have been living up this bridleway for far longer than I have been in the village; They joined the others here a good year prior to my arrival. Many people around know of them, a few even come and chat with them as I do, but far more shun the travellers as an unfortunate and undesirable element. It is a common feeling, I think. It is not as if I cannot even understand it.

Yet Ned and his family are good people. They may not look, or be, that healthy. Certainly their lifestyle is unconventional and their habits perhaps seem uncivilised in what is sometimes a judgemental and exclusive community. Indeed, it is not any kind of lifestyle to which I feel at all drawn myself.

Even so, does it not in many ways exemplify that which makes this country a fine place, worthy of preservation? Not the *way* they live, but that they can make the choice. That acceptance of the eccentric, of the individual and the right to be one. Can we have lost it so completely in this age of vapid, monotonous image and material conformity? Has it simply been ingested and perverted by the empty narcissism of the modern world, so now the closest we may come to being accepted as a "unique individual" is in the self-promotion of our "Story" via social media; A story largely identical to and as mundane as that belonging to everyone else.

I weep if that is the case.

Still, I do believe that Ned's example is a strange sign of hope that all is not lost. For all the less-than-desirable features of their lives, his family seem pretty pleased with their lot. Certainly they want for money; The cost of facilities in a caravan is by no means a pittance and they are not oblivious to the shortcomings of their diet. However, they rarely speak of needing *things*, of desire for new gadgets, gizmos or luxuries. When he earns money doing odd jobs – mainly on local farms – Ned takes pride in the produce he can buy, not in investment in some piece of time-wasting technology or meaningless bauble for their home.

Before you take exception to what I am saying, please do not think for a moment I am setting to on any kind of "the poor are happier" nonsense; That would be as insulting to Ned as to anybody else. It is just that I admire the man's attitude, rather than envy him his lifestyle. Is he actually *happier*? Well, certainly more than I am, but that is a different story. I admire his defiance of the norm, which to my mind is a celebration of a far greater ideal of which we must not lose sight.

I have already approached Darren with my idea and he is not exactly against it. As an outsider himself, he is perhaps more liberal than others in the village. Maybe he is therefore also more conscious of the fact that Ned's involvement on the day of the fair could ruffle some rather vocal and self-important feathers in the community. I too find myself pondering what somebody like, say, Mrs Whitby might make of the whole thing. I like to feel she would approve, but I know that is possibly wishful thinking. In the end, I must simply try and do what feels right to me.

"Just imagining that people did agree," I say after gazing at the leaves for a while, "would you actually be interested?"

Ned prods at the sausage again and pushes out his bottom lip, as he always does when considering something with the maximum level of seriousness he can muster.

"I think I would be, yeah," he says. "I like living out here, you know?" he continues, turning back to look at me and then gazing around at the dripping foliage. "But I'd like it better if I could feel a part of things a bit more too. I know mum would, and Gary."

"That's what I'd like too," I reply.

I leave Ned with a promise to return with news shortly and make my way back down the bridleway to the village beyond. I stop in at the Eagle to confirm Ned's interest with Darren who now seems much more for the idea. We agree to pop up and see Ned together the next day and I head off into the countryside alone.

Like Ned, I need to feel a part of things here, yet I also share with him that need for solitude, for otherness and freedom. This is true even now that my mood in general has picked up again, my energy levels have been elevated and sense of purpose renewed, though the knowledge of the village's vulnerability remains in the back of my mind at all times, coming to the fore with every fresh miserable piece of news on the television or on the radio in the bar.

It is time for another break. There is nothing in life at the moment that makes me happier than getting away from everyone and losing myself in the rolling glory of the West Oxfordshire landscape. I make my way down a wooded slope beside the main road into the village, cutting between gardens and out onto the low grassland that makes up this stretch of the Thames Path. A cool breeze passes through the tall grasses, through the scattered hawthorn and bramble bushes and over the water, teasing out ripples on its placid surface. High above, the warm sun shines, now unobstructed by the rain clouds that have passed on further east.

Birds sing to each other further down near a lock backed by great horse chestnut trees, their mighty boughs creating a thick canopy over the paths that run on the west bank of the river. I cannot name any of the birds by their calls, but stand for a while enjoying the mingled sounds of songs in the trees, the breeze in the leaves and the gentle lap of water below the banks.

The lock must be manned, but I can see nobody as I move on, sticking to the east bank and passing down into deeper grass. A pathway has been cut through, but the towering grasses on either side can sometimes obscure the view beyond. The pathway follows the river upstream through wooded tunnels, dark in the shade of the leafy canopy above. There is an expanse of conservation land beyond, where the grass gives way to low-lying marshland dotted with bird hides.

The sun has been covered again by cloud as I reach the marsh, and I take cover in one of the hides as the heavens open and rain comes down in a deluge. Inside the hide it is still warm, but a shiver runs up my back as I lay my head against one of the pine window frames and listen to the sound of the raindrops hitting the roof. Water drips relentlessly from above the windows and door and I curl myself up on a bench against the wall and close my eyes.

Beyond the window lies the marshland, the river

beyond it and patches of woodland all around. In my mind's eye I pass across them in the rain. My feet skip lightly across the surface of the marsh, through the rushes and onto the river. The rain falls on me and through me and everywhere around me. As I cross the river in leaps and bounds, I find myself flying deep into the woods beyond, ducking and weaving between twigs and branches. Leaves brush against my skin softly, wet with perfect diamond droplets.

I come to rest beneath a great oak; A king among the birch, beech and hawthorn. Gazing upward through its boughs, I can see light refracting through drops of rain as they fall between the leaves towards me. I breathe in, filling my nostrils with the scent of the forest. Reaching forwards, I run my fingers across the bark of the vast tree, closing my eyes and blocking out the sound around me. From deep in the heart of the massive living wooden form I fancy I can feel a pulse; Life beats through everything, into my fingers and up my arms. I move closer and lean my head against the rough skin. The reverberations move into my mind and shake and hold me rigid.

Then all at once they fall silent. It is as if the tree has

suddenly died. Still the rain patters above; Drops fall through the leaves and land on and around me. Nothing else has changed, but I feel lost. All at once I am aware of how alone I am here, deep in the forest. I open my eyes to look for a way back out again, but every former path is blocked solid. Tunnels and gaps between branches have been filled, the foliage seemingly having moved closer together, trapping me.

I am gripped by a sudden terror. I stare back towards the great oak behind, its leaves already turning and falling. Could it be that it had been my protector; It kept me safe when all else that surrounded me moved in. It is gone now and I am truly alone. I stare back at the great wall of forest and feel tiny and insignificant, where once I could have been great; Once when I had been the great oak.

A sound rips through the silence of the clearing and my eyes snap open once again.

My forehead aches where it has been pushing against the hard pine of the window frame. I rub it a little as I look around the interior of the bird hide. It feels colder now. The breeze through the open windows is no longer pleasantly cool. Rain still drums on the roof above, falling in great rivulets beyond the door. The ground beyond is soaking, the earth beginning to turn to mud. The sky over the marshland is dark now, showing no signs of a break in the rain any time soon.

From somewhere out there I hear a sound again.

The sound of laughter.

Stopline Red

The leaves brush against my forehead as I push my face through the shrubs, raindrops trickling down my face. I crouch lower in the undergrowth and wrap my arms around my knees as rain drips from my hair. A shiver runs down my spine.

The girl's voice cries out again, not laughing any more. Is she hurt? Angry? She shouts at somebody else and a male laugh rings out as well.

"How fuckin' far is it? I'm soaked!"

It's the girl.

"What, and I'm not?" The male voice replies. "It's not far."

I creep forwards, pushing small twigs and branches out of my way as I go. The endless dripping of rain from the boughs above sends another shiver through me, but it is a good shiver. One of those that could almost be an expression of comfort; A shiver in which to curl up and lose oneself. I often get these when it rains, peering through windows at the street beyond my room or walking in Oxford beneath an umbrella as the city passes by. In the undergrowth on the east bank of the Isis I stop for a moment to enjoy the sensation.

The voices haven't stopped their babbling. Half arguing, half joking, they are drawing away from me now and I push forwards again. The ground under my feet is not too muddy. The weather has been warm enough of late to resist this downpour for the moment.

Round a bend in the river we go, the others sometimes chatting, at other times merely groaning at the weather. Occasionally I think I catch sight of them, grey and black forms passing between bushes, always following the path that has been cut between the two sides of the conservation area.

I stay within the cover of the foliage.

It occurs to me at one moment that I have no reason to be doing this. Why act in such a suspicious manner? Yet there *is* something about these characters that concerns me.

They seem unlike the people one usually encounters on this route. Yet there is something almost familiar about them as well; The patterns of speech and the choice of words; The tone of voice and their whole attitude. It is something that instantly sets off in me a sense of great anxiety.

I must know who they are and what they intend to do here.

After we have been passing through a flatter area of marshland for a while, where I find it far more difficult to remain hidden, having to rely on the reeds and rushes to keep me from view, we re-enter the woods. I make my way back into the undergrowth, relieved to feel safe and protected once again.

All of a sudden, the pair of figures ahead turn and clamber into the trees themselves. I freeze. Can they have noticed me? Are they aware that they have been followed. I sit, rigid, listening intently, but all I can hear is the rain hitting the treetops above with renewed intensity.

At last a voice speaks again.

"Is this it?" asks the girl.

"It's in here somewhere, seriously."

"I am fuckin' wet through, Den. This better be worth it."

"It is, shut up!"

I allow myself to breathe out slowly. They have not noticed me and it sounds like we are approaching journey's end. I slip forwards, more conscious than ever of the sound as twigs break beneath my feet.

"Here y'are, look!"

I see it too.

Deep within the woods, there is what looks like a World War Two pillbox. Its grey walls and roof may be covered with moss and overgrown with shrubbery, but the distinctive shape marks it out immediately as one of the defences of 'Stopline Red', the decided point of resistance where the forces of the Wehrmacht would be stopped from entering the Midlands.

"What's that then?" the girl asks.

"Some farm building or summin innit?"

"We come all the way out here to see that?"

"Shut up, come on."

I watch as they climb down inside the pillbox,

disappearing into the concrete and moss like snakes in the grass. Best to wait a moment and see if they climb out again before I make my move.

After a few minutes I decide enough time has passed and begin to make my way to the walls of the pillbox, skirting around it at a distance until I can approach one of the gun-slits that has been mostly blocked by a fallen tree. I pick my way across the ground, trying my best to avoid anything that might make a noise. In truth, with the rain falling harder than ever, the sound in the trees above is surely covering my tracks, but I want to take no chances.

The gun-slit is narrow and small shoots that have taken root in the dead tree have created a curtain over it, but I am able to see inside the fortification with enough light to make out the interior.

It is a simple structure, a central concrete pillar with walls extending from it to allow more cover should bullets make it through one of the slits in the side. Beneath one of the walls I can make out a hole in the floor where steps lead down into a lower room, perhaps an ammunition store. The floor is littered with the decomposed remains of leaves and twigs and, in one corner, about fifteen empty, crumpled cans of Fosters. I cannot see the couple I have been following, but through the rain I can make out the echoing sound of voices, more hushed now than before.

They must be on the other side of the central pillar. I glance across at the opposite side of the structure. The gun-slit that looks in from the best angle is uncovered and it is highly likely that my silhouette would catch their attention. I look around again, blinking raindrops out of my eyes.

The door.

The entrance to the pillbox is on the blind side of the central pillar and walls. The steps look to be free of any sizeable twigs or leaves that might give me away. I pause and hold my breath for a moment. My mind swings back and forth.

Is this worth it?

I move my foot and leave my mind behind, shifting round the exterior of the building as the rain grows even heavier above. The branches are doing little to hold it back now. Torrents of water pour down the trunks of the trees. I duck inside the entrance, glad for the shelter, but also for the added noise that masks my movements. Inside, the sound echoes off the walls, reverberating through the stone tomb. Despite the visual impression of decay, the building is as structurally sound as ever. No rain makes its way through cracks or holes.

Their voices echo as well. I stand only metres from them. The voices are so familiar now and I finally realise why. I have heard them before, a memory I wish I could erase. How can they be here, so far from the shopping centre where we first met?

"Den", she says again and I know. I can see his blazing eyes, the aggression surging through him; That moment of hesitation and uncertainty.

They do not belong here.

The fields and trees; The village and the river. They all seem more vulnerable than ever. This incursion from another world, another life that belongs so far away from everything this place means.

The voices have stopped now. There is the rain and the pitter-patter on the leaves. A crack and a hiss and a spent Fosters can clatters against the wall opposite the hidden side of the central pillar. I slip backwards up the entrance passage and out into the woods again.

Out by the riverside I crouch beneath the protective boughs of the trees.

I am too far from home.

I am too far from journey's end.

And everything is shaking as in an earthquake, deep beneath the ground.

Eden

The day of the festival is bright and clear. Thin wisps of cloud hang in a vast expanse of almost perfect blue, the brick walls of the cottages and church glowing with golden light. An almost expectant hush lies over the village in the early morning, save the joyful birdsong in the rich green trees. A few early risers put the final touches to the decorations. Jim at the DIY shop adjusts his bunting, making the hanging sections uniform in width; Mrs Whitby and some of the other ladies of the WI add bunches of flowers to the float into which we have all put so much work.

The most popular float design – put forward, somewhat surprisingly by Mrs Arnham – was a huge representation of Churchill himself. Mercifully, common sense prevailed and instead we have constructed a fairly accurate, if rough and ready, reproduction of Blenheim Palace, flanked by prints of artwork he painted in its grounds. A photograph of the great man, signature cigar clamped in his teeth, sits at the front, surrounded by the ladies' self-made bunches and wreathes of flowers. The entire display has been erected around Darren's van, the use of which he has agreed to give up for the duration. Good chap.

Darren himself is busy in the bar as I arrive from my room. He has been cleaning and re-cleaning the tables and the bar itself. He looks up as I enter.

"Run y'finger over that table," he says, gesturing to a table near the door. I reach down and run my hand across the top, surprised at how smooth it is. Not a trace of its former stickiness remains.

"Not bad," I say, giving him a thumbs up.

"It's taking bloody hours, but I reckon we'll be clean all over by lunchtime."

I make my way to the coffee machine and brew us each a mug. As the machine boils I peer out through the window at the back of the bar. The car park outside is decked with bunting all the way to the fully-erected stage. In front of all this I can see the barbecue and tables that have been laid out for later. Ned is pottering about, getting everything in place.

"Christ," I mutter. "Did everybody get up before me today?"

"Eh?" Darren says, following my gaze out of the window. "Oh, him? Yeah, he got down here just as I was getting breakfast. Seems keen. Says a few others will be down to help out later."

He carries on with his scrubbing while I pour the coffee.

"You sure you're okay with this?"

"What? Them helping out?"

"Yes."

Darren puts down his scrubbing brush and slaps a wet hand on my shoulder.

"Reckon it's the best idea y've had in ages!"

I smile and hand him the coffee.

"Seriously, he's a good lad and if he wants to help out round here I'm all for it."

"Hope everybody else agrees," I say quietly.

"Bollocks to them if they don't," Darren laughs,

picking up the brush again. I smile at this and sip my coffee.

"I'll go see if I can help him out."

"Right y'are," Darren replies and I make my way to the back door.

Ned does not look like he needs much help. Almost everything is in place and he is taking a cigarette break by the wall. He beams at me as I walk over and raises his hand, gesturing at the barbecue.

"Whatcha think?"

"Looks great to me. You need anything else?"

He rubs his chin for a moment and takes another drag on his cigarette, looking around at the tables and chairs.

"I'd say a free pint, but reckon I'll wait till we get going, eh?"

I laugh and sit down. Both of us sit in silence for a while, looking around at the car park. It is so peaceful, as if all the world is asleep and we are the only ones doing or saying a thing. I try to appreciate it, try to let myself sink into the tranquillity and quiet, but the tremor in my mind remains and leaves me on edge.

It has not passed since that day in the rain. My mood

has stayed low and agitated. The face I wear is slipping again and I spend long hours alone in my room, either on the bed, staring at the ceiling and thinking, or gazing out of the window and watching. The grasses on the shrine have died sooner than expected.

I am a lone sentinel, afraid of dropping my vigilance for a second yet equally afraid of sharing my concerns with others. Could they ever understand? Could I ever tell them? Is it fair to shake their world to its foundations, to force them to suspect everything and feel not a moment of peace? This is my burden alone, at least for now.

Yet I long to share it.

"Ned," I say quietly.

"Mm?" he replies, dropping his cigarette to the floor and stubbing it out.

"Do you only spend your time in the country north of the village, or do you ever head out in some other direction?"

"I go all over. We all do, when we're training the dogs."

Ned's little community has an interesting shared

purpose, beyond just making their lifestyle viable and stable: They rescue dogs. Some of the men who live there spend time out finding abandoned dogs, in particular those that are aggressive and appear to have been victims of abuse or neglect. I learned this the first time I passed the row of caravans and was suddenly surprised by a viciously barking dog, held on a lead by a man whose name I later discovered to be Dave.

Dave smiled as I leaped backwards, but instantly tried to reassure me.

"Don't worry, I've got him," he said quickly. "We never let dogs like this run free, not while we're training them. Got to calm them down and earn their trust, you see?"

He explained how they would take these dogs in and try to rehabilitate them, taking away the fear and aggression and hoping that one day they might once again be accepted as pets. He did not mention whether they had yet succeeded, but I found the cause to be a noble one. Indeed, it was this that first made me curious about the travellers and encouraged my later trips to meet and chat with Ned.

"Do you ever see people that don't belong around

here?" I ask, rather embarrassed, but eager to hear his response all the same.

"Aside from us?" he grins.

"You know what I think about that," I reply. "No, people you just don't expect to see. Not country folk."

Ned furrows his brow a little and looks out at the trees in the distance. He sits like this for a long time and I worry he is bothered by the question.

"Sometimes," he says at last. "More recently. Townies and that. Not from round 'ere but Oxford I reckon."

"More of them recently?"

"A few. They go down by the river, drinkin' an' shoutin' an' all that. Keep leavin' rubbish about the place which hacks me right off. I know we'll wind up gettin' the blame."

I stay quiet for a moment and then ask, "Have you ever seen them closer to here?"

"Not yet," he replies, looking straight at me. He heads off to check on the stage again but I stay at my table.

It isn't just me. He knows.

The men with the sound system for the stage turn up about half an hour later and Ned and I help unloading and setting up the speakers, microphones and mixers until about eleven o'clock. The church bells down the road ring to signal the start of the festival and we all head down to the market square to watch the parade.

It's a lovely end to the morning. The streets are full of families, the children genuinely excited about the whole affair, particularly those taking part in the school march. I worried that young people no longer cared about things like this and I am happy to have been wrong.

After the school children come the WI ladies with Mr Churchill. The beaming grin on Mrs Whitby's face and the light sparkling in her eyes make all my effort on the float worth it, as do the huge cheers and applause from the crowds of people lining the street. There are more cheers then for the local football team, all four Aunt Sally teams, the art club, the church bell ringers and the various local shopkeepers all decked out in appropriate – and occasionally inappropriate – fancy dress. Darren even gets in on the act, staggering down the street while deftly handling eight full pint glasses on a tray, to much laughter and applause. Bringing up the rear is the predictable motorcade of tractors and steam engines, but such is the joy with which they are received I find myself unable to roll my eyes or even laugh.

Another ecstatic ringing of the changes pours from the church at twelve o'clock and the parade breaks up down on the sports fields at the end of the road, where numerous stalls and tents have been erected, selling everything from wooden bows and arrows to locally-produced honey, cider and ale. Ned, Darren and I mill around the field for about an hour, occasionally stopping to remind people about the barbecue and music at the Eagle, then make our way slowly back to the pub through the wooded grounds of the old abbey, plastic cups of cider in hand and smiles on our faces.

Back at the pub, Dave and Ned's little brother Charlie have arrived and are pouring coals onto the barbecue. Darren and I leave Ned with them and head in to reopen the pub. A few revellers are already at the door and within moments we are pouring pints and toasting the great success of the day so far.

For the first time in days I find myself contented and,

yes, happy. As I gaze around at the ruddy faces and the bunting and the smoke starting to rise from the grill outside I can let all my worries go, at least for these few precious moments.

The bands kick off at two o'clock, with a group called Auld Yellers blasting out a wall of poorly tuned guitars and vocals that feed back horribly through the microphones. One of the blokes from the sound system suppliers fiddles with the mixer to rein in the squall, but it is having its desired effect anyway, drawing more people up from the fields and into the pub.

Fairly soon the barbecue is a hive of activity, burgers and sausages flying off as quickly as Ned and his companions can get them done. I find myself splitting my time between helping them and manning the bar with Darren. Pretty soon we are running low on glasses and have to turn to the boxes full of plastic cups until somebody can be found to go and do the washing up.

At some point in the afternoon Ned scoots off to get more meat, buns and napkins and comes back with his mum who looks uncomfortable at first and gladly takes the opportunity to hide in the kitchen, washing up the steady rotation of glasses. I pop in to see her in a rare quiet moment and bring her a hotdog and glass of beer. She has lightened up and even says she will come and join the festivities later, which pleases me. I can understand her reticence and her feeling of not quite fitting in, but I really would love for her to join Ned and the others in making themselves more a part of the village.

The best part of the afternoon for me is when I catch sight of some of the village old boys having a good laugh with Ned outside by the barbecue, drinking together and making him welcome. It may be wrong of me, but I feel a certain sense of achievement at seeing one of my friends being accepted. I feel an even greater sense of pleasure and no small amount of surprise at realising that I actually do have friends.

At about five o'clock the party is raging all around us. Darren charges downstairs to change a couple of barrels and I draft in Dave to man the bar. I tell him to do his best as I slip away to grab the phone that has been ringing on and off for half an hour.

I lift the receiver.

"Hello, the Eagle!"

"Hello there, mate."

It is Dram. The world around me slows to a crawl and my insides squeeze up into a knot. Everything falls silent save the distant crackle down the line.

"How you doing?" Dram asks.

"I – I'm good, Dram," I reply, hoping he will not hear my feelings in my voice.

"You having a party?" he asks.

"It's a village festival," I say, trying to drag my village face back on and hide what is beneath.

"Sounds busy."

"It is."

"You good?"

"Y-Yes."

"Good."

"Um, you?"

"Yeah."

. . .

"Good."

"You're settling in then? I was wondering."

"I think I am. I like it here."

"You like it?"

"Yes."

"Good."

…

…

…

…

"Okay, mate," Dram says. "You take care of yourself. Was just checking up. I'll be in touch soon."

I stare at the mirror behind the bar, my face cut in two and distorted by a bottle of Jack Daniels.

"You too, Dram," I whisper.

He hangs up and I slowly lower the receiver back onto the phone. My breathing is heavy and my head feels cloudy.

"Hey!" Dave shouts as he slaps me on the shoulder just a little too hard. My mind cracks, rage surges through me and I wheel round on him, for the briefest of moments curling my hand around a bottle beside me.

He is shocked and as the red washes from my eyes I

realise how I must look. I let go of the bottle and breathe out slowly.

"Are...are you okay?" Dave asks, still looking shocked.

"I'm sorry," I say quietly and then force my face into an exhausted smile. "I'm sorry, just so wired at the moment."

"Oh," he says, his face relaxing somewhat. "You good to give us a hand?"

I nod and follow him back into the maelstrom at the bar.

It is nothing to the storm inside my head.

Fuse

By ten o'clock the whole village is a mass of revellers. Every one of the numerous pubs is full, the Eagle included. The final act hits the stage at ten past and lets rip with a triumphant set of blues and rock classics. I make my excuses and wander off into the streets to get some air. I need the space; I am still on edge after Dram's phone call.

Out in the cool air of the evening, away from the noise and clutter of the pub, I let the breeze blow across me and listen to the gentle rustle in the leaves of the trees on main street. I sit down on a stone bench that juts out from a wall rough with age and covered with moss and lichen. The stone feels cold against my bottom, but I don't mind.

The main street is quiet. The sounds of revelry drift across from near the market square and Eagle Road, but there are no pubs here and the stone buildings are peaceful. Mrs Whitby's shop has a glow in its windows at the far end and a few other homes show signs of habitation, but otherwise all is dark.

Closing my eyes I think back to the moment I first arrived here. How strange it had been starting out again in a place so completely at odds with what I had experienced in the past decade. Many would have doubted that I could fit. Dram warned me before I flew out of Jakarta –

Damn, the memory takes me straight back to the call in the pub, the hand curling around the bottle, the look of shock. I shudder at the thought.

This place could be home, I think. My manners have changed. My speech and even my gait. My attitude as well? It must have changed. The warmth I feel for the village's people and the horror at its vulnerability. The effort I make every day, the energy with which I throw myself into every facet of life here.

I tried to go home once. A month ago I made my way back to the town of my birth. My parents still live there somewhere, but it was not to see them that I went.

Parts of the town were much as I remembered from my school days. The long pathway from the Copse secondary school I had attended still wended its merry way down through the estates on the hill, beneath the conifers and along the hedges of that dirt path overlooking the vast mead that bisected the town. At the foot of the hill it crossed the railway tracks and further on it met the town centre.

Yet the old Lanstrom Country Store was gone, replaced by a phone shop. The hours spent chatting with friends outside its door before we parted company for the evening were gone with it. I left the centre as quickly as I could. That upsetting mixture of the immediately familiar with the crassly altered shook me, made me feel like an alien in the one place I once felt I belonged. Over the hill near the old chantry I went, down into the woods beside the cricket field.

There, beneath the great old oak beside the same old brook I found the place that once meant the most. That last summer after we left school had been spent there, playing with video cameras, staging fights, clowning about together in the warm sun that broke through the leaves and boughs above and dappled the brown earth of the hollow with speckled gold.

It looked much the same as always at first, but as I moved closer I saw that somebody had carved a swastika into the bark of the tree and sprayed it with black paint; The warm brown soil was scattered with bottles and cans and used condoms; Fag butts and crisp packets had been piled into a mound in a burned-out tear in the base of the trunk.

What did I think then? There was anger, certainly, but sorrow more than anything. Even this hallowed ground had fallen; The gates of heaven were beaten and shattered and strewn with the broken remains of bottles of Stella. The wolves at the door had taken the throne and all they could think to do was make it into a latrine. Did they even know what it was, what could be done with it?

I wept.

"Oi!" a voice called from behind me as I wiped the tears away. I turned to see a group of four youths behind me. For a moment I remembered that day in Oxford and adrenaline began to flow in my veins. They were the same. They looked just like them. They had those same sardonic expressions across their faces and those same listless eyes. I guessed they were in their late teens, just as we had been, but worlds apart.

Two of them demanded to know what I was doing in their place, as though it had not once been mine as well. They had that same aggression in voice and posture I had seen in Den. They threatened me.

"This is our place. You gonna hang around all day?"

I stood as still as the great oak behind me and said nothing. They were big – all youths seem to be now. They all stepped forwards as a group and sized me up.

"There are four of you," I said. "You're bigger than me and I see you mean to hurt me."

They stopped and looked at me, those eyes still seeming to stare right through me, except for one boy who appeared confused.

"But I have my hands. I have my teeth and nails. And I have more rage than you can imagine. You might beat me to the ground, beat me half to death. You might even kill me. But I promise you that at least some of you will go home scarred for life. So leave now."

Long, long moments passed as they stared at me, mostly in disbelief. The leader still struggled to maintain a look of sneering contempt, but the rest were clearly unsettled.

It worked.

They left. It took a long time, but there was a change in those eyes. Uncertainty and even a small measure of fear. It came first to the boy at the back of the group and gradually spread through them all. They walked away making promises to be back later.

I left town an hour later knowing that I would never return.

A smash and a tinkle of glass pulls me back as it showers across the rough pavement. I look up the road towards the shops to see a group of black shapes staggering out into the street. The echoes of laughter bounce down the street off the rough-hewn stone walls of the houses and businesses. I stand and begin to walk towards them.

Who the hell is this?

Drunken revelry or no, I have never heard of the villagers getting like this. By the sound of the smashing a window has gone and up that way it can only belong to somebody I know.

A mixture of anger and new-found determination rising within me, I quicken my pace and bring myself up to full height. I feel in my pockets for something to use as a weapon. Only my keys. Barely good for scarring, let alone anything more convincing.

They are moving, these interlopers. Whether they see me or not they must know that the sound has not gone unnoticed. They turn and bomb off down New Mill Lane, in the direction of The Stag, first one and then the rest, whooping hysterically as they go. I have time to see them round another corner by the pub as I arrive outside Mrs Whitby's shop. Glass is strewn across the pavement and the front window is gaping wide.

For the briefest of moments I consider my options before concern calms boiling blood and I turn to the shop. The door is locked, as one might imagine, so I climb through the window.

"Mrs Whitby?"

Nothing.

"Mrs Whitby? They're gone. Are you there?"

"Is it you dear?" a quiet voice quivering with fright

calls back. She is upstairs. Gradually I coax her down and she stares in horror at the window, shivering in her old-fashioned nightgown embroidered with bluebells. The breeze blows through the shop. I say nothing, waiting for her to make the first move. She breaks down in tears and I have to help her into her easy chair.

Lament

A warm cup of tea calms her nerves, but she never stops staring at the broken window. I let her sit for a while as I sweep up the glass below the sill and search for something to block the hole. I call The Eagle, but nobody picks up, doubtless engaged in mopping up the after-party and dealing with the remaining punters. Now I am gone they must be short-handed.

After a long while, Mrs Whitby manages to speak again.

"I just told them to go."

"Who?"

"Those children. They were making so much noise, drinking in the street. I waited for them to go, waited for somebody else to come out and deal with them, but nobody did."

"You should have called me."

"I didn't, I didn't know what to do. I was so scared."

"I'm sure you were."

"And the language. You should have heard them."

I put down the dustpan and look back out of the window at the dark street. A few locals are milling about, but nobody seems to notice us in here, or the shattered glass on the pavement outside.

"Do you know them?"

"No, I've never seen them before. They weren't from round here, I can tell you that."

She curls up in her chair and shivers. The night air is not cold, but I get her a blanket from the back room and she wraps herself up. For a long time we say very little. I drag down another blanket from upstairs and hang it over the window, clipping it to the curtain rail with clothes pegs and string.

"Was it all worth it?" she asks.

"The festival?"

"All of it. Everything we did."

I slump down into a chair opposite her and take a sip from my cup of tea.

"I was in the Royal Observer Corps, you know."

"You've never told me."

"No. I suppose I'd never thought about it."

"A great responsibility," I say and smile a little. She doesn't smile back.

"They were amazing, those men. Sat up in towers and places all over the country from north to south, calling in reports and we would put them all together and map them out. I've never understood how they could be so precise."

I smile again and this time she responds in kind.

"We would get all those reports and some clever bods would collate all the data. Then we'd put it all on the table and on maps and call it through to Fighter Command."

"I love this kind of thing."

"Do you dear?"

"It's like a different world."

"Yes," she says, looking down at her tea. "Yes, it was."

"Heroes," I say, hoping it will not sound too stupid.

"Yes," she says again, not raising her eyes from the cup of tea.

"All of you."

"Because you knew what you were doing back then. You knew why. Everybody knew why."

She glances up at me and then at the blanket moving gently over the window as a breeze picks up.

"It may seem silly to people today, that idea of fighting for freedom. I know it has become so very popular to dismiss it. But we knew what it meant."

"Of course you did."

"I can still see them all now. The whole lot of them, me as well, sitting around those tables and waiting for the calls to come in. It was like a day at the office really, laughs and jokes and all that, but always so focused when it mattered. We were so young, but..."

She looks back at the window and then at me.

"And now you look around and wonder why we did it all; Why we bothered."

I let my small smile slip away and look her in the eyes. There is such sorrow there. Perhaps it has always been there, either hidden away or just something I have never taken the time to notice. This woman and her fantasy of a world that mattered. I get it now. To live in a dream when all the world is beyond hope, is there anything there to misunderstand? Have I not been doing the same in my own way?

"The freedom to do what?" she asks and I'm not sure if she is asking me. "Is there still a young person alive who cares or even knows?"

"I do."

"Yes," she says, looking at me wistfully. "Yes, perhaps you do, my boy."

I lie back in my chair and look up at the ceiling, tracing its antique cracks as they crawl around the room.

"All that sacrifice," she says. "All that worry and fear and heroism and strength. For what? It makes you wonder, doesn't it?"

"It does."

"It makes you wonder what purpose God had in mind when he put us here."

None. No purpose at all.

We put Him in heaven to give ourselves one.

Mission Statement

My antipathy towards religion is not without its foundation in reality. I do not dismiss it without extended thought, just as I do not ignore the things it has brought that I would not do without.

This land in which I live, for which – even unwittingly – I have fought in my time away and strive to preserve now was founded on religious ideas. Every land was, even those that, like this one, have abandoned its unquestioning mysticism. The ideals and aspirations at the core of national character and its extended political thought grew from the start out of those less rational belief systems and the conflicts and debates that they encouraged – even as so many laboured to discourage them.

I would not do away with the aesthetic vestiges of those beliefs either. Much of the colour and vibrancy in the world, indeed I would argue the lion's share, has been created explicitly to support and celebrate such beliefs. The great churches and cathedrals of Europe and the New World still inspire me as works of art and acts of devotion; The garish hues and scents of the sub-continent with their music and ascetics and staggering pantheon of gods; The Greeks and Romans with their tales and temples and the Norsemen with mighty Yggdrasil; The festivals and dances of the Malay Archipelago; The great mosques of the Islamic world; The beauty in form and considered architecture of Japanese Shinto. Every one of these makes the world a place of value beyond the bland and the facile. The gadgets and selfies. The dull empty narcissism of modern life.

Yet not one of these impresses me with a sense of spiritual importance; Not one speaks of a higher truth. They speak only of the potential beauty and poetry of human delusion. It is a delusion that in and of itself is neither good not bad, merely there, and yet it has darkness at its core as well. When delusion takes the form of determined certainty of one's righteousness over all others it goes beyond all sense of playful enjoyment and celebration to rape and corrupt the human spirit. At heart maybe that is what lies beneath the surface of all these great works without which I would find the world dull. It is a thought both troubling and confusing.

Such intense certainty of a group's innate correctness of belief combined with the certainty of supernatural support drives mania and fanaticism. Why can fanatical belief not be content to merely be that? Why are people so animalistic and idiotic that we cannot ascend beyond the need to spread, control and force the ideas we take to be true across the planet?

To state, as many do, that we are just animals ourselves is no kind of answer at all. While all genuine thinking men may ironically question the truth of the name *Homo sapiens*, it stands as correct; We *do* think and *are* capable of extended rational analysis. And is that not the ideal for which any system of belief, rational or otherwise, strives – to elevate ourselves above other animals by the power to marshal base desires by means of intelligent thought?

And yet we forever find ourselves slipping back into the same old patterns, the easy road of higher powers and superhuman justifications.

And it is all nonsense.

I will never stop somebody thinking what they want as long as they respect the right of *every other person* to live and believe whatever they choose, but at times I cannot help but think that the world would be a far less fractured and painful place were people to realise how naïve an explanation for all that exists is a sentient, omniscient and omnipotent higher power that for some reason takes great interest in and umbrage at the actions and opinions of every single individual on Earth.

Protection; Defence; Union. These are the ideals I hold to be true and for what they may lack in ritual and baubles they more than make up for in the celebration of logic, enlightenment and reason, at least to my mind. A shattering of that union, of those ideals, truly is irreparable. At this time of all times we need it more than ever, surely. Being confronted by outside forces so utterly removed from our hopes and beliefs – that word again – should cement our structures and systems, not rupture.

It is to that end that I stand on a hill overlooking the

river valley. The land gently slopes away from me, rolling its way to the Isis as it curves and meanders between the hills, a shimmering mirror of light in a landscape of earth browns and leaf greens. High above hangs the azure sky, not a cloud as far as the eye can see. The warmth of the sun drapes itself on my back and for a moment I close my eyes and am lost in it.

A few miles below in the valley lies the village. The tower of the Anglican church stands out in the centre near the market square, its sand coloured walls golden in the sunshine. A bus heading towards Oxford departs the stop in front of the church and heads east. I watch it as it trundles down the road, sometimes visible, sometimes obscured by the rows of trees that run out of the village. Down near the lock it crosses the humpbacked toll bridge and finally makes its way onto the Oxford Road. This is the village's most vulnerable point.

From the south there is less risk. The road that runs down past the abbey grounds merely wends its way happily off further west into the smaller hamlets that lie beyond. Unless we are caught in a flanking manoeuvre – unlikely –

that is perhaps the lowest on our list of priorities.

The northern approach to the village is less easily defined in terms of its risk level. From my vantage point up here on the hill I cannot clearly see the bridleway that leads into the woods beyond the village, the path on which Ned and his comrades have their community. The farmland beyond would offer plenty of opportunity for people to hide and plot, but the tiny villages that lie in that direction represent a minor threat, many of them even more rustic and traditional than ours.

I sit down on the grass and pull my OS map from my knapsack. Spreading it out on the ground I look at the village. It lies alone in the farmland and vast tracts of conservation areas that run down to the river and beyond, across to the reservoir and further south to Cumnor and Eaton. Through it runs a single road that could be considered major, an artery connecting it to Witney in the west and the mass of tiny roads and buildings that is Oxford to the east. I take a pink highlighter from my knapsack and draw a line the length of it, from the toll bridge into the heart of the ancient city. I would have preferred red, but the folk at

Staples told me you couldn't get highlighters in that colour, so I have to make do.

Ned is late, but I am unsurprised. He is a busy man and the dogs need a lot of attention, particularly when they are newly taken in. He does not drive and they only have a couple of motorbikes, neither of which belong to him. He is doubtless walking to meet me on the hill, which of course is what I did.

I reach over to my bag and pull out a small packet of sandwiches I have made for the day; Tuna, cucumber, tomato and a dash of hot pepper sauce. Delicious! I munch my way though them, basking in the warm sun and sipping from a canteen of water I bought at the charity shop on New Mill Lane. It is a WWII original with a dent in the top where, so they claimed, a bullet had struck. I am dubious about this, but the thing looks the part and feels reassuringly solid. It could even serve as a weapon, should it come to that.

Ned appears after about half an hour, strolling out of the undergrowth. He is dressed as always in a Motörhead t-shirt and worn jeans, a knapsack of his own on his shoulder and dog in tow. It is a vicious looking thing, doubtless one of the new arrivals. It strains at the lead and seems to leap at almost anything that comes into its line of vision. I have never been a huge fan of dogs, far less since that night in the sewers, but I do not mention it as he arrives and takes hold of the dog's collar.

"Nice up here, isn't it?" I say in greeting.

"Beautiful. I think I've been up here before actually."

"That a new one?"

"Eh? Oh, Mario here?"

He pats the dog on its head and for a moment its eyes stop bulging.

"Came in about a week ago. Still pretty aggressive so I've got 'im on the lead. Good dog though, I reckon."

He leads the thing over to a nearby tree and ties it up. It barks for a moment and then, perhaps realising that it is going nowhere, sits down and starts licking its own balls.

"You eaten?" he asks.

I nod and reach into the bag again, pulling out a hip flask. I offer and he takes it gladly.

"Thanks. What is it? Whisky?"

"Aberlour."

"Eh?"

"The distillery. Try it."

He does and probably takes too much as I can see him manfully straining to hold back a cough. He grins and hands it back. I take a smaller swig and feel the warmth seeping down my throat and into my chest. Ned seats himself on the ground looks at the map spread out in front of us.

"What's the pink?"

"I wanted red."

"Red?"

"The colour."

"Not pink?"

"Why would I want pink?"

"Well, yeah, but..."

"I know it looks absurd."

"No, it's – "

"It does. Anyway, beside the point."

"Yes. So..."

"Mm?"

"The pink?"

"Weak link, Ned. That's the gaping hole in our wall."

"Oh."

"Yes."

"Mm."

"Right?"

"Absolutely. What?"

I point down into the valley at the trees by the lock where the bus out of Oxford is passing.

"Our main point of vulnerability. That's where they can get in. The north concerns me a little but your people have that road sewn up. West and south are clear, aside from the incursions around the river, but the eastern approach is wide open."

Ned doesn't speak, just looks at the valley and then back at me.

"Okay. Who are we talking about?"

I look at him and I'm sure he understands the expression on my face.

"When you agreed to come up and make these plans you understood why, right?"

"Yeah. To stop those little twats from town messin'

things up and breakin' windows and the like, right?"

"Right. Exactly. From *town*. And where do they get in?"

He looks at me blankly for a moment and then slowly points back into the valley. I nod slowly and swig from the hip flask. He seems to be thinking; His brow is furrowed and he is licking his lips a lot.

"So what do you want to do? Hold up the buses?"

"Jesus Christ!" I exclaim, probably more loudly than he would like. "No, but *that* is where they're doing it, that's where they're getting in! That's where we need vigilance, Ned."

He raises his hand to calm me.

"Okay, wait...wait. Just supposin' we come up with a plan and watch out for 'em, just supposing we actually have the time to do that, why there? Why not set up some neighbourhood watch?"

"I don't want that *filth* on the streets," I say as quietly as possible, well aware that my gritted teeth make this sound far more aggressive than I intend. "I want them back in their own neck of the woods, fucking up Blackbird Leys or whatever other unfortunate place has to give them shelter. I do not want them to so much as set foot on the pavements of this village. It is beyond them and above them and I *will* defend it, Ned."

He says nothing, just sighs and looks back down into the valley.

"Give me a week. Just one week. You said yourself it's been happening more and more of late and I saw the look on your face at Mrs Whitby's."

"Poor woman."

"There will be more, Ned. Are we to just sit back and wait, or stand up for people too afraid to admit what's coming?"

He drags himself to his feet and walks down the hill a little way from me, taking the hip flask with him. He sips at it, less this time. I watch him and begin to fold up the map.

"Okay," he says at last. "What do we do?"

Dua

There is a dog that snaps at me first, a rabid, snarling thing with fur torn away around its face. It takes me a fraction of a second to know that it will be upon me before I can reach any of the men. Two of them are still seated, not five metres from me, but further back are two more. One is dragging a machete from below the wooden box he is using as cover, his eyes wide with fear. The fear is good, for fear makes for haste and error. The other is calmer, at least he lacks the panicked expression of the other three. I catch the tiniest of glints of light on metal from his hand. Whether it is a knife or a gun I cannot know. The single light source is a yellowed striplight set behind wire and metal bars on the ceiling. There is a door.

Forget the door.

The hatch finishes its slow crash to the floor beside me and with that time speeds up and the dog lunges. I catch it in the jaws with my hand and barely notice its teeth cutting into the skin as I leap forwards, swinging the head backwards and lifting its flailing body from the ground. My blade tears through its throat, arcing blood to the left, the direction in which I throw myself. There is a box there I can use as cover in the event the fourth man has a gun. Of course, if he has a gun, the box will do nothing but confuse his aim and only then for two shots at most.

The dog and I crash into the box, papers and a steaming cup of coffee flying from it as it tips under our weight. As soon as I hit the ground I fall forwards into a roll and bring my blade upwards as I right myself near the closest of the men. I miss the throat and tear a gash up his face, through the side of his nose and on to his right eye. In the split second it takes me to pass him and reach the second man I watch his eye slip from its socket and his mouth round into a severed scream. Two of our eyes meet and all I see is horror.

The next man falls more easily – I do not miss the throat. My confidence rises for the moment and then the flash comes and the crack of thunder and the bullet hits me and I am dead.

The smell fills my nose, a smell from years ago. My mother sipping water from a bottle, my father and brother discussing the football results. All around the lot of us hangs the gorgeous aroma of the forest. That smell of soil and leaves; The sleepy feeling as the smell of the bark on the trees, wet with moss and the recent rain, enters my nostrils.

"Come on, team," my father calls, a contented smile on his face. "Only five miles to go."

We two boys protest the distance, but in time we will come to realise what a gift has been given. The group of four marches onwards, light filtering through the green canopy above, turning patches of the brown soil golden as it hits. Not one of us utters a word, each lost in the warm embrace of the forest.

Such times were these, such times I have lost. Yet with the merest sniff of the undergrowth, all these memories wash over me like an ocean, like a tsunami of nostalgia. They may now be the smells of foreign, alien roots and leaves, I know not, but how different can an environment be? From the moment humankind opened its feeble mind in East Africa, from the time it first ventured forth into the Levant, have not the trees existed? Chlorophyll has never altered its scent. The sun on leaf is eternal, at least as far as this talking ape can know.

As spunked the raven, so fell the rye, when apple cherry flowed in rivulets as atrocious as the pastor's morning squelch. When the economisance ran on the river, so did the man climb ever higher to signs of wastrels in the abode above the swan. Petitions to the heavens as worms to warm pools of tears. Sanctified in the act of torture the bracken snapped and heels clicked and a boot stamped on everything. Red rum, red mum, deadcum feddumb asreachedin the night of apocalypse asreachedin thetimes ofthejourney beyondthe happy dayslonggone weretheyandlong gonewas she she she thequeen hope thequeenwho cangive andtake andbleed forallandsundryforaneternity.

Crack. Crunch.

Snap.

A low...dull...hum. No, a whine, like when somebody leaves a television on with the sound muted. It is almost impossible to detect at first, but gradually it grows out of the absolute silence around it and begins to fill all the dark spaces with its static groan. For a few minutes – or perhaps hours, no time yet – there is nothing more, but slowly another vibration joins the whining. It is a dull, rhythmic pulse, deep and warm. It is the sound of blood being pumped through arteries and veins, heard from inside a head.

Light begins to grow on the horizon. It is a horizon with no sky and no land, no up and no down, but a horizon it remains. It is the point of meeting between was and was not, something and nothing. In here is nothing, all-enveloping and peaceful, but empty, save the throb of blood. Now light comes and light is something. The something pushes on the edge of nothing, ever so slowly forcing its way inside. The darkness in the distance grows to a milky white, until the centre begins to glow more intensely, a raging force bursting through. Daggers of light shoot out from the heart of the darkness like crepuscular rays and tear it to shreds.

The world is a blur. The blinding light fades slowly, but nothing is in focus. Distant shapes and images move, but everything is lost in fog. From deep within the mist and rumbling, distorted sound echoes, like thunder heard from under water. The next time it is a little clearer, it takes shape, finds separate sounds to give it character.

"Wake up."

Bloody Terror

I have of late finally become aware of my cycle. As regular as clockwork as it may be, I have never been able to identify each step and each agony as simply as I now do. It begins as always with irritability. The smallest aggravation is elevated to the level of an unbearable itch, an itch I can no more scratch as I can rip the man from the moon and smother him with a used continence pad. Loathsome and hateful intrusions, both imagined and objectively existent, tear at my mood and my behaviour with the unceasing bloodlust of rabid dogs. Every slight and every inconvenience stabs like a blunt dagger at my mind, contorting the view of the world seen through my eyes into a vision of scum and shit. This twitching mania segues into the darkest of dark thoughts, the world falls black and the future becomes as much an unknowable horror as it does a blank, bleak void. All is devoid of hope, of chance of improvement or any possibility of amelioration. And then, perhaps three of four days from the start of the process the darkness wrests control from all else and pure hopeless sorrow slides across the scene, a thick pall of choking smog through which neither the glimmer of stars nor the light of the sun can penetrate. Tears fall like a brutal winter drizzle, without intensity but all-encompassing and insidiously pervasive. Tremors and shudders and absolute fragility render me incapable of action, and so I remain until the phase shifts and the briefest hint of buoyancy slips in and carries me above the gloom, at first a true blessing, but swiftly intensifying to the point of manic idiocy. What was first irritation becomes pure unstable rage. Blood could flow. Faces could be smashed to rags. And through all of this uncontrollable hatred and yearning for slaughter seeps an undercurrent of misguided hope. The pain and rage and sound and fury give way for the moment to action and creativity and desire and even a modicum of sense. Until the cycle swings around on its inevitable wheeling through the galaxy.

That is why I must use this time.

I slip onto the bus and make my way to the top, just a few seats behind them. There is no need to be closer and being further away would serve no purpose. They make every intention as clear as day through their ceaseless, inconsiderately loud chatter. How I treasure their lack of decorum now.

Their goal is clearly the village. One imbecile even speaks of their shattering of Mrs Whitby's window and few even attempt to chastise him for the glee with which he does so. Den is here; I hear his name repeatedly and the moron is cackling away with the rest. Their overall target is unclear although the pillbox is mentioned in passing. That is good. If they are planning to leave the village for quieter territory our mission will be more easily completed.

We are nearing the toll bridge when one of them hits the button. I start. In the village I could disembark without notice. Out here by the river I would be stepping off with them, all alone. My mind races as I watch them drag themselves to their feet and make their way to the stairs. I cannot get down now, that much is clear. The bus crawls to a stop and I watch them wander off in the direction of the river, slipping down the steps beside the bridge.

The bus pulls away and I hit the button immediately. I grab my phone and shoot a message off to Ned, then I leap up and scramble down the stairs to the bottom of the bus. The bridge passes, then trees and bushes. Every second they are getting away and I am running in the wrong direction. I dive from the bus the moment it stops and charge back, my lungs busting as my feet pound on the pavement. Ahead I see the bridge – I could cross it but instead slide down the bank to the near side of the river. There is a narrow tow-path that cuts through the undergrowth and then out into the open. I duck down at the end of the wooded section and peer across the fields on either bank.

Nothing. No – wait, there is something. A flickering glow of white light some distance away on the far bank. The screen of a smartphone. I can make out dark shapes moving with it now. They are quite far ahead of me, but that is good. I know where they are and where I need to go. About a kilometre upstream is another lock and that is the only point for miles where one can make a crossing without the use of a boat. I am certain they will not be crossing anyway as the pillbox is on the far bank and I must assume that is their destination.

I slip along the bank, confident I will not seen in the dying light of the day and from such a distance. The river meanders as I make my way upstream and I veer away from it at times to make up distance on my quarry. One skip across the lock and I am back in the leafy surrounds of the conservation area. Pausing briefly to send Ned my location I still my breathing and listen. Birds sing quietly, the river babbles and a gentle breeze passes through the leaves above me, but I hear nothing else.

I check my bearings. I cannot be more than half a kilometre from the pillbox now so whether I am still following the youths or am between them and it depends largely on their speed. I have seen no sign of them since crossing the lock, but they cannot be far away. I listen again and at last hear a murmur of voices from the track to the north. I am ahead of them.

Ducking further back into the undergrowth I watch them pass. That girl is there again, along with Den and a couple of the others from that day in the city. Two of the boys carry shopping bags stuffed with cans and bottles. The girls exchange meaningless non sequiturs while banging away on their phones. Apparently somebody is a slag and a cow while another is well two-faced.

I wait a short while and then move on, following from a distance. As expected they cut in from the path near the pillbox. I am about to do the same when I hear it. From behind me there comes a panting sound, quiet at first but rapidly becoming more audible and definitely coming closer. I turn and see what I have feared since putting this plan into action. In spite of all my suggestions to the contrary, Ned has brought his new dog. The shock factor will be undeniable, but I hate the bloody thing and am unconvinced of his ability to control it.

I am right. Ned is nowhere to be seen and the dog is making no move to follow the youths into the trees. It is tearing straight at me, eyes wild, teeth bared. I do not wait for Ned to catch up, nor do I care any longer about being seen by the youths. I turn and dive under the trees, scrambling forwards, branches ripping at my hair and around my face as I begin to run.

I have just got to get away from the thing. It is right behind me now, moving with a serious purpose and a look – glimpsed in the last terrified glance I allow myself – of absolute madness on its face. I run. I do not think I have ever run so fast, nor with such desperation. Flashes of the sewers and the men and the glint of light on chrome pass before me through the whipping twigs and thorns, but nothing compares to this. The arcing blood, the look of horror; An eye leering towards me from the side of a head, a crack of reverberating thunder and stab of pain. And always that thing behind me.

I dive to the ground. He is on me. I draw my arms up over my eyes and breath dies in my windpipe, yet nothing happens. The panting is suddenly past me. A girl screams. I open my eyes and roll around on the floor. The thing is ripping through the mud and fallen leaves and the youths are scattering like pigeons. Den drops the bag of lager cans and pelts off into the darkness. The others are gone too and the dog is following. I drag myself to my feet, blood thumping in my ears and my heart pounding its way through my chest; Adrenaline is surging through my veins and every sense is firing at a thousand percent.

I try to hold my breath again, listening for any sounds out there in the dark of the trees. There are barks, not too far away, then they stop and there is nothing. I look behind me. Ned is nowhere to be seen. On all sides there is nothing but the wooded grove, and on the edge of vision the black outline of the pillbox.

Moving very slowly I begin to edge forwards to where the shopping bag lies on the ground. Pushing it open with my feet I peer inside; Two six-packs of Fosters, a lighter and a packet of cigarettes. I reach down to pick it up and then my eyes catch movement in the darkness.

The faint flash of light on a pair of eyes.

The creature flies out of the undergrowth and is on me. I raise my arm. Its teeth snap down around my elbow, shift further down the arm and lock in place. We fall backwards onto the leaves and mud and then the pain finally shoots up my arm and into my brain. Somehow I manage to stifle my cry a little, but the beast bites down with more force and I can feel the skin breaking. Instinctively I swing my left arm and catch it across the nose with my fist. The dog holds on and I beat it across the face again. And again. And finally it lets go and jumps back.

I fall in the opposite direction, pivoting my body so that my right leg wheels round and lands with its foot in place to run, but before I move another muscle the thing's teeth are in my calf, ripping through the trousers and flesh. Terror rises in me and then something snaps and all I feel is rage. I wheel around again and bring the heel of my left boot down on the back of the filthy beast's neck. There is a beautiful crunch of bone and cartilage and the teeth are gone from my leg. The dog rolls over, growling no longer but whining in terror.

Terror is right.

I am on it before it can get back to its feet. My left boot powers down onto its throat, pinning it to the ground. As it wriggles beneath me I raise my right leg, blood trickling down over the sock and boot, and bring it down with every shred of force I can muster on the ribcage. I stamp again and the thing stops moving. Then again and there is another satisfying crack. Then again and again and again and again and again and again and at last something gives way, my foot punches through and something curious and gelatinous pops out.

I could stop. I could leave it, but the madness has taken me and I do not want to. I stamp again and again, bone and offal and blood and meat flying up at me. Again and again and again I power the foot home until at last I am hitting earth and leaves matted with gore.

I stagger backwards and stare down at what remains. But for the head it is barely recognisable as an animal. My boots are encrusted with torn flesh and sticky with thick, dark blood, most of it not my own.

Suddenly back in the moment I look around in a panic. Has anybody seen me? Did they see? Good god, do not let Ned be nearby. I see nobody, but that does not mean – no, I must be safe. They cannot have stayed with this vicious thing running amok.

I have to hide the beast though, as well as patch up my own wounds. I will need to get to a doctor too. God knows what the animal was carrying and I have doubtless made things worse by putting my foot through its gut. I reach down and grab the remains by the hind legs. I make to pull it away towards the pillbox and discover that, rather nauseatingly, I leave the top half behind. A long rubbery stretch of entrails slithers along behind it like some obscene tail.

I take hold of the throat and slide both halves away across the ground. Then I kick the mud and leaves over the patch of gory destruction. Hopefully it will rain some time soon. I pick up the two halves again and drag them back across the mud to the pillbox and down through the entranceway.

The damp mossy air of the bunker hits my nostrils and for the first time I realise that the stench of viscera is everywhere. I absolutely reek of the stuff and there is no way I can go to hospital like this. I cannot really even risk heading back to town in such a state. That can wait though.

I pull the dog down into the confines of the central bunker. It will probably be a while before anybody comes so I can leave it under the sodden mattress in here and let it rot. Hopefully by the time any other explorers turn up it will be unrecognisable.

"What the fuck are you doing?"

I freeze. The voice is so loud inside the echo-chamber of the pillbox, but she is probably just whispering.

"What?" I ask quietly.

"What is that?"

Her eyes widen and she stares up at me.

"Oh my god..."

"It...I...it attacked me."

"Oh my fu-"

"It attacked you too."

She says nothing, does nothing. Nothing but stare at me in absolute horror. Gone are that arrogant swagger, the sneer and the sardonic tone; A single, quiet whimper is all that comes out now.

"Look," I begin.

"Are you mad?"

"What?"

"Are you some sort of mad person?"

"No, I-"

"How did you do that?"

She finally looks down at my legs and as her mouth widens I brace myself. The scream bounces off every wall of the bunker, seeming to rise to a chorus and multiply itself, a hundred voices blending in and piling up. I have to stop it and as my mind boggles and swims I find myself walking over and planting my hand over her mouth.

She recoils and swings at me with her arms, her painted nails clawing at my face. I reach about with my other hand for anything and finally it closes around a cool, heavy, unopened bottle of liquor.

Tiga

Dram is kneeling over me, a look of concern on his face. There is some blood on his shirt. I am not sure if it is mine or somebody else's. It is quiet though so the whole thing must be over. Turning my head I can see the bodies of two men in the corner of the room. The chrome outline of a handgun glints at me with a cheeky wink from beside one of them. It reminds me to feel pain and I wish it hadn't.

"Ouch," I say, rather pathetically. I cannot do much more. There is an eye staring at me, an eye that has been detached from the split face in which it once lived and worked.

I am shaking. The room is quiet like a bomb and as Dram moves to touch my arm, the shifting of his shoes on the hard concrete is like the deep splintering rumble of an earthquake. I flinch at the sound and curl up.

"You're gonna be alright, mate," Dram says,

completely incorrectly. I am not going to be alright. This has not happened in a while but I know what it feels like. The warning signs have been there for a few days and I should never have come on this mission. I could have jeopardised the whole thing. As it is, my mind is to be the most serious casualty.

Somehow he gets me home. The bullet in my shoulder hurts until my whole arm goes numb and cold. I limp along, leaning on Dram's arm, the whole world buzzing and crackling with electricity, wrapping me in razor-wire. I feel so fragile and so weak, like the smallest sound could break me.

The streets above nearly finish me off. The crashing of metal on metal, the grinding of machinery and engines; The voices echoing down alleyways and the thump of music from the buildings around us. Every sound beats against the side of my head and I shiver and shake at the agony of it all. Even when he bundles me into the safe house apartment I continue to shake, balling myself up in bed and enveloping myself in blankets in spite of the thirty-six degrees of humming humid heat. The fan above does nothing anyway, besides letting out a rusty whir that sends me shivering again. I pull a pillow over my head and lie there, feeling rivers of sweat seeping into the bed clothes and mattress. Perhaps if I do this for long enough I will just die and everything will be better.

The doctor comes some time during the day. I do not remember his face. I barely see him at all. He shoots something into my shoulder and gets to work cutting out the bullet. I am not sure if I am supposed to feel pain but I feel nothing physical beyond the shivering and shaking and the excruciating scream of metal on metal every time he drops one of his instruments back onto the tabletop. I wince and screw up my eyes and feel those long, thick tendrils burrowing through the front of my brain, clouding everything and making me drowsy.

After he is gone I lie on the bed and feel like cracked glass. Any little push could send the crack right through and I would shatter. The sunlight from outside seeps through tiny rips in the sickly-yellow curtains that bathe the whole room in a thick urine-coloured haze. Somewhere in the building, people are fucking. Their moans and groans throb through the walls and through my head. I slide back under the covers and pillow and sweat until I fall asleep.

So pass two weeks in which I am incapable of venturing from the safe house. Dram comes in sometimes and by the end of the first week I am able to shuffle out to the living room to talk to him, a pair of earplugs in to dull the sounds that still send tremors through me.

Dram says things are bad. The mission was not a success, despite the cell's destruction. Nobody important, apparently. The body in the pipes was removed and hidden, but it seems word had already been sent out about it before we arrived, so the whole thing had been a waste of time and resources. A damaging waste of time and resources.

I am not to blame he says. There was nothing else I could have done and everybody knows that. He says. In all honesty I am incapable of caring and I tell him as much, in the agonisingly slow and laborious way that seems to be all I can manage. He knows it and I think we both know that we both know that I am done; Fully out of the strength needed to be useful and fresh out of fucks to give.

When Dram is not there, I cry. It comes on suddenly,

without warning and I lie on the bed with the sweat-covered bedding over me and weep for the hopelessness of it all. All I have for company during this time are my sobs and the sex noises from the walls.

As a result, it comes as no surprise when Dram suggests that I leave the country. He makes it sound like it is just for me, but I know this is hard for him too. We have been together for a long time and been through a great deal. He has seen me like this before and been patient, but every time I have seen it chip away a little of his resolve, a little of his resilience and a little of his patience. I agree with him and he sets about getting my ticket and packing in order.

By the day we go to the airport I am on the mend, but still a long way from top condition. He tells me I can wear a new face, that I can be anybody I want. I know he is wrong.

I have no face. The only thing I had was a purpose to hold me on track. It is gone now.

"So build a new one," he says.

I manage to raise my hand in a wave as I walk through security. He raises his and smiles.

Equilibrium

"I am so, so, *so* sorry, mate," Ned says. He's standing by the door with his cap in his hand. It is one of those flat farmer numbers, a little incongruous given his age and the Iron Maiden shirt, but it is a fairly classy tweed-looking thing.

I do not reply. I want him to realise how serious things have become and, at any rate, I am finding it hard to say much at the moment. I turn and look out of a picture window that overlooks a park. There are some children down there, playing with a football and shouting to each other. The sky above is a thick overcast. It might rain later, which would be nice.

The blank-faced doctor has just finished reviewing the grotesque embroidery he made out of my leg yesterday and is giving us some time to chat while he does some paperwork. From the moment he came in his facial expression has barely changed. His eyes display no sign of surprise or interest, though I am certain he does not get quite so thorough a mauling case often.

The dog savaged my leg far more horribly than I realised out by the river. There are three distinct sets of teeth marks and one in particular went very deep. With the added infection risk caused by me putting my foot inside the thing, I am lucky I have yet to lose the leg. Obviously I have not told anybody about that, but regardless I have been under close observation for a couple of days, with repeated return visits booked.

When I left the pillbox I ran as quickly as possible to the river and, without really thinking – my mind was capable of little at that point – I dived in and swam to the far side. By the time I clambered up the bank, most of the filth and blood had gone, leaving only a gradual flow from my own wounds.

I made my way back along the bank to the road by the toll bridge to wait for a bus to town. There were few other passengers but those who were there gaped in horror at my torn trousers and the dripping blood. One elderly lady was kind enough to offer me her scarf to stem the flow from my wounds. I tried to make her keep it. It was an expensive-looking piece and would certainly be irreparably ruined, but she insisted. We tied it tight around the worst part and it was already soaked crimson before we made it to town.

From the bus station I got a taxi to the hospital and was admitted fairly quickly, which was reassuring. Clearly the nurses on duty were even more concerned about infection than I was. Under the doctor's instruction my legs were utterly drenched in antiseptic fluids and other creams before they shot five syringes of rabies vaccine right into the wounds. To say it was painful would be an understatement, to say I comported myself admirably would be a lie.

"I wish you hadn't brought it," I say at last. Ned nods and looks really rather sad. I wonder briefly whether his sadness is more for the dog's disappearance, but then realise I am being unkind. Ned is a good man and a caring one too. Seeing him with his family has shown me that.

"I didn't think. I thought he was ready."

"Well..."

"Does it...does it hurt?"

"It's sore. It aches a bit, but it's not so bad now. It's just infection that we have to keep an eye on."

"I don't know if –"

"They've shot me with rabies stuff, so –"

"I am *so* sorry."

I glance back out of the window. One of the children is on the floor, holding his leg. The others are crowding round him.

"Where is it now?" I ask.

"I don't know. He ran off, I guess."

"Same as those kids."

"Did you see 'em?"

"Yes. They were terrified. I doubt they'll be back. That at least is something."

"I suppose."

"You going to try and find him?"

Ned shrugs and squeezes his hat in his hands.

"I don't know. I don't really want to see 'im again. I'd feel, you know, sick or somethin'."

I stay quiet, but try to give him a smile. He brightens up a little at this.

"Better to leave him then," I say. He nods in reply.

"You gettin' out of 'ere soon?"

"Doctor says I can leave once I can walk comfortably. I'm going to wait an hour or so."

"You want me to wait?"

"No, it's okay. I think I'll walk into town for a while. I'd like some time by myself. Can you tell Darren I'll be back this afternoon? I'll need a pint or two."

He smiles and says he will, then leaves me alone.

I do not really know if I'll need a pint. My head is not well. It is certainly not as bad as it has been in the past, but those thick tendrils are there in my frontal lobe, gently teasing the edges of my mind. Everything depends on which way this goes. I do not want to be laid up in bed right now. Part of me needs to return to the woods again, to check on things. I need to reassure myself that everything is in order.

Ned has brought me some fresh clothes and I change into them, binning the rest. They are utterly ruined anyway and I want shot of the things. My boots have been cleaned and dried by one of the nurses, which was very nice of her. They are still warm when I put them on and I flex my toes inside the clean socks. It feels good.

The sky is darker by the time I make it to town. There is that smell in the air that comes before a storm and the horizon to the west is black as pitch. I walk slowly along the high street to Queen's Lane and make my way inside. It is a lovely little lane, flanked by high walls of sandy stone at the back of the colleges. In the dim light below the grey sky it has a slightly melancholic atmosphere. There are few people here and I am free to run my fingers along the rough, beautiful walls. It makes me smile a little. As the rain begins to fall I slip beneath the covered bridge at the intersection with New College Lane and pull my raincoat in around me.

It is dark beneath the archway, dark and comforting. I shiver, though the air is not cold. It makes its way up my spine and I smile to myself. It is another one of those wonderful shivers that seem to warm the rest of my body and bring me deeper inside myself to a place that is safe and reassuring. The rain grows in strength and raindrops begin to make their way down the walls of the college, dripping from the overhang above me and falling into the road.

My mind drifts to the river again and to the dim muddy

clearing beneath the trees. The rain falls there too and washes across the killing ground. It drips from the gun slits in the pillbox, runs down the steps to the interior. It trickles into the lower bunker beneath the mattress and fills it.

A flash of lightning and a distant roll of thunder bring me back. I pull up the hood of my raincoat and turn down New College Lane, beneath the cold watchful eyes of gargoyles and the high walls of the colleges. Ahead, Hertford Bridge straddles the road and I duck down the alley to the Turf, squeezed in below the old city wall that now streams like a weir.

It is early and the pub is quieter than usual. I slip beneath the low beams of the door frame and seat myself in a dark corner from where I can still watch the rain beyond the entrance. Lost in the darkness, a pint to hand and the exquisite sound of the rain hitting the roof above, I am at peace, if only for a moment.

It is a new war, and for these streets and lanes and alleys and low timber beams I fight. My first battle may have been won. I cannot know what will happen, but my terror and vulnerability subside in the deluge beneath these hallowed walls and arches and spires. I find myself wishing that Dram were here to see me and wonder what he would think. For so long we fought the good fight over there, protecting those for whom the war did not even seem to exist – just as I do now. It is their peace and ignorance that must be preserved, for they are weak in their way. I do not resent it; I admire the tenacity in their unseeing pride and in the deceptive air of simplicity with which they live. What greater cause could I have than this?

The rain shows no sign of stopping, but I have work to do and loose ends to tie. I make my way out to Broad Street and down to George Street where I can catch the bus, just as I did all those months ago. This time those undulating hills and the flat expanse of the valley are lost in the mist of rain that batters the windows of the bus. I trace drops as they run down the panes and breathe easily.

I get off the bus at the toll bridge and make my way down to the river. The rain has eased a little, but more is on the way. Lightning flashes in the distance and the rumbles are getting closer again. My boots slosh through puddles and fresh mud as I skirt the edge of the reservoir and keep as close as I can to the cover of the trees. Occasionally I stop for a rest and to avoid the rain as it strengthens again in bursts. I hide beneath the hawthorn and weeping willows and enjoy my shivers. The tendrils in my mind have slithered into the background once again and renewed purpose is keeping them there.

It is as I am approaching the trees near the pillbox and preparing to duck beneath the canopy for shelter that I catch a glimpse of fluorescent yellow that brings me up short. The policeman is emerging from the undergrowth and glancing around for somewhere to shelter. He sees me and nods. My mind races; *What should I do?* There can be no other reason for him to be here, yet the absence of police tape or greater numbers of officers reassure me that, for now, I am safe. I walk over and join him beneath the tall tree under which he has taken cover.

"Bit wet for a walk, isn't it?" he says, not exactly smiling.

"I'm trying to get back to Cumnor," I say, in as friendly a manner as I can muster. "Been out all morning but got caught in this. I've been sheltering in a bird hide up that way for more than an hour."

"Worst luck, eh?"

"Had my lunch with me," I grin. "Wasn't so bad. At least I'm doing it for fun, not working!"

He laughs and then grimaces a bit.

"Tell me about it."

"What are you doing out here in this?"

"Missing person. Haven't seen a girl around, have you?"

"A girl? No."

"Her friends called about it. Were out here a couple of nights ago and got split up. When they tried to find her they drew a blank."

Thank god. Nothing yet.

"I haven't seen anyone," I say. "Although I've only been out this morning."

"Well, if you do, give us a call. She's dressed up for a club apparently, so you won't be able to miss her. Kids these days, eh?"

"A club? Out here?"

"Classy!"

I laugh and promise to call if I see or hear anything. He wishes me luck on my way to Cumnor and says he will be heading back shortly.

That settles it. The rain has surely done its work on the remains of the dog and there is no chance he would have failed to check the pillbox. The cat remains in the bag and the wool in place over the eyes. I breathe a sigh of relief and make my way farther downstream to a more sheltered area beneath the thick canopy of trees in one of the conservation areas by the reservoir.

I have to go back.

I cannot wait to see if anything happens. I must make sure everything is secure. Every single screw needs twisting and every bloody stain needs scrubbing. This battle cannot be less than a complete victory for all that is right and good and proper.

The pillbox is flooded when I arrive. The rain has sloshed down into the interior and soaked through the mattress over the lower chamber. I drag it back and slide down into the dark. She is still there. Her caved-in face gazes up, one straggling eyeball dangling off to the side prompting a dagger of lightning up my spine, but I have moved beyond all that now. His eye and her eye and every single fucking torn eye are gone and all that remains is the mission.

I am staggered by how well I am holding all of this together. Peering down into her shattered face and broken skull, ankles-deep in decaying dog guts, I feel nothing but pride in the blow I have struck for the cause. I can see them all now. Ned with his mother and brother, Mrs Whitby, Darren; All of them must see why this has happened. The walls of the village have been shaken and the sky has darkened, but here is the ray of light; Here is the mortar and brick and plaster.

I know I need to move her. There is no way the next visitor is going to miss the trapdoor and the longer she is missed the more likely it is that police will return in greater numbers. But when and where to go? Dragging a battered, dripping hunk of meat will take effort so it can only be done at night. Then there is the destination to consider. I mean the river is hardly ideal and who would want to pollute it with this? I could always bury her, but that would need tools. I guess Jim must sell shovels and the like and I doubt he would be too surprised if I bought one. Any place around here would probably be okay, as long as I plant her deep enough.

God. She looks awful now. There is barely anything left of her upper jaw, if that is what one calls it. The bottle shattered her top row of teeth and then punched on through the bone. It was hard work, I can tell you. Do you know how strong the skull is? It would surprise you. Life may sometimes feel fragile but when you actually go about the business of ending one it can take far more exertion than expected. The bottle lies there in the hole too, smashed to pieces.

I cannot find the dog's head. I know it is in here somewhere, but the water and gore are hiding it. The light is bad too.

Fuck the dog. It is hardly the issue. Even here in this land of soppy morons nobody is going to give a damn about the shredded cadaver of some stray. A stray girl is another matter.

Burial

Jim does have a shovel. He is odd about selling it though. He looks at me long and hard when I ask for the thing, as if he already knows.

"What do you need that for then, eh?"

"Eh?"

"A shovel?"

"Digging."

"I know, but, you know, you don't have a garden..."

"Do I need a garden? I have more important things to be getting on with, Jim."

"Are you okay?"

I wince at this. He suspects something, yet he has no idea why he should really be afraid. It rips me up inside to know how completely delusional people can be.

"Do you like your shop, Jim?"

"Um...yes."

"Do you not hear the foundations shaking?"

He says nothing and I know I have him. He knows I have hit the nail right on the head.

"There are bigger things for you to worry about," I say, "than a man buying a spade."

He says nothing, but takes the money and offers a confused half-grin.

"You alright?"

"Fine. I'll see you later."

"Right you are."

Something makes me swing by the Eagle on my way to the bus stop. Darren asked after me during my trip to the hospital and I want to put his mind at ease. It certainly would not do to have him paying more attention to my activities than usual, not right now. I also need to get out of the rain for a bit and maybe change into something dry.

"There he is!" Darren exclaims as I walk into the bar. "How's the leg?"

"Sore, but worth it," I reply.

"That mate of yours said you were out chasing off kids from town."

"Yes, I was. We were."

"It's a bit weird, but good on you. That poor old lady up the road'll be happy, I reckon."

I nod and sit down by the bar. Darren pours me a pint and we chat for a while. My mind drifts now and again, floating off to the woods, down by the bar stool to the shovel and even off across the world to the sticky streets of Jakarta, Bangkok and Kuala Lumpur.

I should call him. This is the right time to do it.

"Can I use the phone?"

"Eh? Oh, right. Local?"

"International, but I'll pay it all back."

"Right-o, I've got casks to change anyway. Mind the bar as well, will you?"

Dram picks up after three rings.

"Hey."

The noise in the background suggests he is indoors; The horns sound distant and muffled, the whir of a ceiling fan is audible when he pauses.

"Hello, Dram."

"This is a surprise. Are you okay?"

"I think I am. I feel different now."

"That's good, as long as you feel good. What have you been doing?"

"I can't really say right now, Dram, but it's good. It's a purpose, like I used to have."

"Great!"

"Like we used to have."

He pauses for a moment, as if he is weighing up what to say. To be honest, so am I. When I called I had something in mind, but now I am not so sure. Will he have me back out there? Do I have the right to ask, yet can I take the chance of staying here if things get serious?

"We did, eh?" he agrees.

"Dram," I say, lowering my voice. "What if – what if I said I wanted to come back?"

That pause again. This time I know what he is thinking.

"I don't know," he says in an apologetic tone. "It's a hard one. Things are getting more serious by the day here."

"All the more reason. Dram, I – I want to try and make up for it." *Wait, what am I saying?*

"I get it, I do. Let me think about it. When are you planning to come?"

Good question. What am I even thinking of, suddenly making a plan to go? This is supposed to be a fallback scheme, a last resort. I have work to do.

"I don't know. I was just thinking about it. Wondering if you'd be open to the idea."

"I'll get back to you, eh? I like the idea, really I do. I miss having you here. Why don't you focus on your project for now and we'll talk about you coming back some time soon? Does that sound okay?"

"Yeah," I reply, relieved that he has not given me a chance immediately.

We say goodbye and I hang up. I feel a little disappointed in myself. I have got all this work I have planned and I know this sense of purpose has held my mind in check, but out of fear – yes, that is what it is – I have courted betraying it all. The village needs me, even if it does not realise it; I am the sentry on the battlements, the sentinel on the frontier and I have a duty. Escape is not yet an option, if it ever can be without betrayal.

I pick up the shovel and leave by the back door.

She is starting to stink, or maybe that is the dog. It is both, I am sure. The first maggots have begun their feast, pushing their way through the face and across the dog's spilled guts. I wonder if it is really necessary to do this yet, when they might be bones in a week, but I know it is too big a risk. When she does not turn up, the police will certainly be back. Her friends will surely be around as well when the police report back that they have returned empty handed. This has to be done and sooner rather than later.

The rain has almost stopped, but the ground is very soft, so digging proves easier than I have feared. One large hole should be enough, some distance from the pillbox to be safe. There is a perfect spot within a mass of hawthorn trees. It takes a bit of effort to climb under the low branches and getting the bodies in will be difficult, but nobody is likely to venture this far through the woods and the thorns should deter them. I dig until my hands are sore and my back is screaming for a break, but I have only made it half a metre deep. I wonder how deep is enough. I would like to get down a metre at least. The hole does not need to be particularly wide; I can curl her up into a foetal position to make it easier.

I dig for a while longer and get maybe eighty centimetres down, all across the width of the hole. The ground has become harder down here and I decide to call it done. It is as I crawl out the other side of the hawthorns that a sight greets my eyes that freezes my blood.

Den.

He has come back. I suppose it is no surprise that he has come, but he is between me and the pillbox and he is heading towards it. There is something about his face.

Not serious.

Something like sadness. Something I know.

Still, better that I am here at all. If he had come a couple of hours earlier, this could all have been over. My eyes widen as I suddenly remember that I have not pulled the mattress back over the lower bunker entrance. She is exposed to the world and even with the dim light, that smell will draw him in.

My fingers tighten around the shovel as he reaches the

door and slips down inside.

How long do I wait? It will surely only take a minute for him to find her and then there will be no other option. Yet if I wait for that very moment of discovery, he will be distracted by the horror of it all. That moment could be enough.

I leap to my feet and sprint across the wet leaves of the clearing, reaching the steps into the bunker at the very moment a cry of utter terror echoes back at me. Diving into the bleak halflight I bring the shovel swinging upwards from where it hangs beside my leg. Den turns almost in slow motion, his eyes so wide they could almost fall from the sockets.

I am back in the storeroom beneath the pounding streets of the city and everything is flowing like treacle. The air smells of moss and corpse and rot and rain. I see the horror in the man's eyes and horror in Den's at the same time. My blade swings in from the right and catches the man in the lower jaw, tearing up through to his eye.

My shovel flies up from below.

Behind him I see the glint of daylight refracted through

a single raindrop that detaches itself from the top of a gunslit in the wall. It falls past the backlit foliage, onto the moss that covers the inside of the ledge. I can smell the damp earth and hear the rustle of the leaves beyond the door behind me.

The shovel tears through Den's head, ripping a whole chunk free and he tumbles backwards into the hole in the floor, barely a sound escaping his lips, save a pathetic moan. The lump of head hits the side of the inner partition and falls to the floor with a squelch.

It is silent, but for the breeze in the trees, the occasional pitter-patter of rain and the sound of my breathing. I stand still and stare at the moss in the gunslit. The water still glistens and I can still smell the green and the earth.

A quiet groan comes from the lower bunker and I raise my body up to its full high. My breathing slows, my heartbeat with it. I tighten my fingers around the handle of the shovel again and prepare to drop into the hole. And then I hear it.

"Hello?"

It is coming from outside. A single projected call, then

a lower stream of speech. A burp of static follows it, the unmistakeable sound of a walkie-talkie being clicked off. My feet barely able to move, I shuffle to the entrance and peer out to see the fluorescent shimmer of a police officer slipping through the trees.

The jig is up. There is no way I can take him as well, not with others doubtless on the way; There is no way he will fail to smell the whiff from the pit in the pillbox. My only chance is to get away before he can get here. Tensing my body, looking away to the route through the trees to the path by the river, I take hold of the walls on either side of the stairs.

One breath. One deep breath.

I launch from the entrance and fling myself forwards on my toes. I make it halfway across the clearing before I hear a shout, another quarter before another splutter of static from his walkie-talkie. I drive onwards into the rough twigs and thin branches of the undergrowth, thorns ripping through the skin of my arms and face until I hit the waterside and veer right. My heart is already pounding in my chest, lactic acid building in the muscles of my legs, but

I must not stop. I tear onwards, leaping from one side of the track to the other to avoid patches of wet mud and to force myself ever onwards at greater speed. I dare not look back, but throw anxious glances up at the ridge of the reservoir to my right, expecting every second to see yellow jackets.

I catch sight of them as I reach the first lock and slip through the gate. There are two of them some distance away at the crest of the reservoir walls, one pointing down, the other speaking into her radio. I have little time and I know it. My only hope is to reach the Eagle before anybody figures out who I am, to grab my passport and the briefcase of money and skirt the village until I find a bus stop away from the centre. Then to the centre, the bus station, Heathrow Airport and then out to Dram. It is a tall order, but I have made a life of scaling mountains and have reached every summit so far.

Across the lock I duck behind the trees that flank the river and then cut out across the fields towards the village. Beads of sweat are streaming from my forehead and stinging my eyes. The wounds in my leg are sore and probably opening up again beneath the bandages. I do not care. All that matters is the room above the Eagle, the shrine watching over my lost home and the money and documents that can keep me free. By the time I reach the edge of town, I can hear a distant siren. I cut left by the abbey grounds and nature reserve, avoiding the high street and market square altogether, finally coming out of the trees a mere hundred metres from the Eagle.

Darren is nowhere to be seen when I arrive at the pub and I slip up the stairway round the back unnoticed. My hands are shaking so hard that I fumble the key in the lock for a few agonising seconds before the door opens. There is no time to pause or take stock. I drop to my knees and pull the briefcase from beneath the bed, briefly check that my passport is still inside and turn for the door. Then I stop for a second, glance back at the shrine of broken dreams, pick up the vial of dust, plant a kiss on the pile of dying leaves and finally make my way out.

The sirens are clear now. The police are in the centre, probably asking Jim and Darren and anybody else they can find what they know. My gut tenses up as I imagine Mrs Whitby among them and for the briefest of moments I feel an intolerable sense of shame. For all my good intentions, I know how she will feel; This nice young man with his sense of propriety and honour; This outstanding pillar of the community, so dedicated and capable.

Should I surrender? The idea has merit, but I baulk at it all the same. For all the dishonour I have brought upon myself in their eyes, I did it all for them; They who could do nothing to protect themselves; They who still live and work beneath a shadow they can barely see, one that can now move unchecked, without any watchman at the gates. The watchman should never surrender. The watchman can still watch from afar, can still make the world safer for them and their way of life, if only indirectly and at great remove. Never again may he smell the air on the common, never again see the golden warmth of the sun on the ancient forbidden stones, yet through his watch, through his struggle and toil they may still endure.

"Where are you going?"

The voice shakes me from my stupor. I turn and see Darren standing there, near the door of the pub. He is looking me up and down, his eyes widening. He knows, or at least he is starting to understand.

"Oh my god," he whispers. "It *was* you."

"Darren," I start to say, but he is shaking his head and edging backwards towards the door. The muscles in my legs tense again and my knuckles go white around the handle of the briefcase. He is only a few metres away and he is no fast mover. The briefcase has a metal edge around the join and the handle is strong enough to support a swing. Yet this is Darren and if I have earned – and now lost – a friend in England, it is him. Time stands still as he ever so slowly moves away from me and my mind races from possibility to possibility before finally calming with acceptance and resignation.

My last act in this village will be honourable.

I turn to leave and am hit in the side by the full force of a flying body and a flash of fluorescent yellow. The last thing I hear as my head hits the ground is Darren's cry.

Face

The lawyer has the appalling nerve to submit a plea of insanity on my behalf. It is rejected immediately on the grounds that I have refused to support it, but the insult burns inside for days.

They trail them all in, one by one. To a man they have nothing to offer but anger and betrayal. For them I can see it is only repaying like for like, but I reply with no apologies or pathetic excuses of my own. The outcome is clear from the start and I will not lower myself and my mission to begging. Martyrdom suits me far better, whether they recognise it or not.

Ned seethes on the stand, clearly angrier about the death of his foul beast than the slaughter of the interlopers. He becomes so animated when talking about my recruitment of him – "grooming" he calls it, clearly having learned to read a newspaper – that the judge warns him to calm himself or stand accused of contempt of court. All the same, the man makes no attempt to dismiss Ned's claims and only raises his voice to overrule the objections of my counsel. When they finally finish with Ned and he leaves the stand, he shoots me the deadliest glance I have ever known. I do not give him the satisfaction of returning it.

Darren hurts me more than any other. It is not his anger at being "deceived", but the sorrow that is palpable every time he speaks. There are moments as he speaks of the festival preparations and the Churchill float in the parade when I sense tears behind his eyes. He rarely looks in my direction, but when he does it is not with hatred, but with something almost approaching pity. I do not know which is worse.

There is a big turn-out in the court for the verdict; Newspapers and other media have leaped on the case and are gobbling up every moment for broadcast across the nation. Of the village folk there are few who have made the journey. I am told by the judge as he makes his final comments that my actions have left them devastated and their community irreparably fractured, but I doubt it. The village will endure, watchman or no. One day another will come, I am sure of that.

The jury – to the surprise of absolutely nobody at all – delivers a unanimous guilty verdict and there is a rather embarrassing cheer from the public gallery. Even the judge appears to find it a bit much and shoots an aggravated glance at them, but I do not think anybody cares. Then he gives me a double life sentence without chance of parole, which suits me fine. As the officers stand to lead me away he asks me if I have anything to say for myself. I have considered this quite carefully during my long nights in the cell and look up at him with a face as serious as I can muster.

"We are not made of sugar candy."

He regards me with curiosity, but says nothing, just nods to the officers who come and take me from the silent courtroom.

The War

I watch it all from my home as a guest of Her Majesty; The planes and the shootings; The robberies and the protests; The beheadings, rapes, burnings and declarations of war; The nightmares of Paris and Brussels. Every new horror within and without brings with it the return of the dreams and the torn faces with gaping eye sockets. Every day in the prison continues like the last but darker and more oppressive.

They let me keep the vial of dust but it no longer offers any solace or protection. Now it serves as nothing but a reminder of what I have left behind. Yet still I know it was right and this is just a continuation of my struggle and toil, the promise I made to the world and its people. I had hoped its memory would live forever, but as the weeks and months pass it vanishes from the news, to be replaced by greater fear and a greater sense of hopelessness in those among the populace who bother to pay attention. I resign myself to having no part in it and simply turn my attention to books.

My fellow inmates steer clear of me for a while, but eventually some come round and we spend time talking. Some of them are open to my ideas and listen intensely as I offer the justification for what I did. Few agree with the methods, but many accept the overarching reason. All share the helpless sense of impotence in such a time and with each new report from the outside world our collective dissatisfaction grows. The gatherings and conversations grow more frequent, until the authorities – perhaps under the mistaken belief that we are planning insurrection – place restrictions on group size that essentially end the exchange of thoughts and ideas. I retreat again into a world of reading, hoping that in the words and opinions of greater men some comfort and understanding can be found.

It is spring again when a guard comes to my cell and calls me out.

"You have a visitor."

I follow him to the visiting room in a state of confusion, wondering who could possibly have cause to see me. It may be Dram, a possibility that fills me with equal amounts of hope and fear: Hope because it means there is one on the outside who remembers and perhaps understands, fear because his judgement may still be harsh and the loss of my last connection to society is something I cannot bear.

It is not Dram. Seated on the other side of the table is Mrs Whitby. She has dressed in her best clothes, those she saves for church and that she wore in the parade the previous summer. She sits in contemplative silence and as I enter she raises her head and gazes into my eyes. Perhaps it is my imagination, but for a second I am certain I see the briefest hint of a smile. Then it is gone.

I sit down opposite her and say nothing. I feel that same gnawing sense of shame in my gut and wait for her to make the first move. For the longest time that is how we stay; Each looking into the eyes of the other, neither willing to speak. Then she glances down at her handbag and fishes inside it for something. She draws out a small iced cupcake, turning it from side to side in her hand and staring at it. Then, with a nervous smile, she looks up at me, slides the cake across the table and leaves it there.

I reach out and take it.

For Hanh and all her patience.

Printed in Great Britain
by Amazon